"**A**re you pregnant?"

"Nope," Giselle said, playing with her rice. She couldn't look at him directly. She concentrated on her food.

Pete sighed. "I don't know if this is bad news or good news. I don't know how to feel."

Giselle inhaled raggedly. "I know. Maybe relief is a good word."

"I don't know, I am not particularly relieved." Pete mused. "I guess it is a good day for you then. You got two scholarships that you have been working for since forever, and best of all you are not pregnant."

Giselle blinked her eyes rapidly.

BABY FOR A PRYCE

BRENDA BARRETT

JAMAICA
TREASURES

Baby For A Pryce

A Jamaica Treasures Book/May 2019
Published by Jamaica Treasures
Kingston, Jamaica

This is a work of fiction. Names, characters, places, and incidents are either the product of the author's imagination or are used fictitiously. Any resemblance to an actual person or persons, living or dead, events, or locales is entirely coincidental.

978-976-8247-70-4
Jamaica Treasures
P.O. Box 482
Kingston 19
Jamaica W.I.
www.fiwibooks.com

ALSO BY BRENDA BARRETT

FULL CIRCLE
NEW BEGINNINGS
THE PREACHER AND THE PROSTITUTE
AFTER THE END
THE EMPTY HAMMOCK
THE PULL OF FREEDOM
REBOUND SERIES
THREE RIVERS SERIES
NEW SONG SERIES
BANCROFT SERIES
MAGNOLIA SISTERS SERIES
SCARLETT SERIES
WILEY BROTHERS SERIES

ABOUT THE AUTHOR

Books have always been a big part of life for Jamaican born Brenda Barrett, she reports that she gets withdrawal symptoms if she does not consume at least two books per week. That is all she can manage these days, as her days are filled with writing, a natural progression from her love of reading. Currently, Brenda has several novels on the market, she writes predominantly in the historical fiction, Christian fiction, comedy and romance genres.

Apart from writing fictional books, Brenda writes for her blogs blackhair101.com; where she gives hair care tips and fiwibooks.com, where she shares about her writing life.

You can connect with Brenda online at:
Brenda-Barrett.com
Twitter.com/AuthorWriterBB
Facebook.com/AuthorBrendaBarrett

Chapter One

Just one more lap. Giselle thought as she ran around the track. One more step. One more push. She stopped. She couldn't make it. No amount of pep talk was going to get her get her there. Her legs felt as if they didn't belong to her.

She was tired and drained, inexplicably so.

"Come on, Gis," Kurt urged her on. He jogged past her and then turned around. "What's up with you today? Feeling sick?"

"I don't know." Giselle sat down in the middle of the track and stretched. "I cannot go another minute. I might be coming down with something."

Kurt frowned. "That's been happening a lot lately. Are you subconsciously choosing medicine over tracks?"

"Why would you say that?" Giselle frowned. "I train every day!"

"And you are progressively getting worse." Kurt snorted. "You knocked over five hurdles yesterday. Your time has dropped to what you used to run in high school, which was way past a minute. I have a hunch that this is more mental than physical."

"I don't know. Maybe. I am just not feeling it." Giselle panted. "I just want to go home, have something to eat and crash."

"Are you sure this has nothing to do with the brand-new shiny scholarships that you got today?" Kurt sneered. "Are you sure that you are not listening to the sweet, serene call of med school, and now you have mentally exited the will to do tracks?"

"How did you know about the scholarships?" Giselle glared at Kurt Yu, her coach and now tormentor. The scholarships were supposed to be a secret until she decided to reveal it.

Kurt stopped jogging on the spot and folded his arms. "Everyone in the Science building is celebrating your accomplishment. Giselle Pryce got not one but two scholarships. She is a genius and so pretty too. Oh, joy and delight!"

Giselle chuckled. "Look happier for my success, Coach."

"I look like this all the time. I do not have a smiley face. Deep down inside, a generous part of me is rejoicing at your success. Deep, deep, down."

Kurt slumped beside her on the tracks and groaned. "You were doing so well. We could have gone pro. Now you are going to be a sports doctor. Where's the fun in that?"

"I didn't say I was going to take up the offers." Giselle watched as Kurt shook his head from side to side and pulled his fingers through his overlong curls.

He was half Nigerian, half Korean, and he was tall and muscular, not too heavy or too thin, he had the slanted eyes from his Asian father and thick curly hair from his African mother.

He mocked her, repeating what she said in a high-pitched exaggerated facsimile of her voice. "I didn't say I was going to take up the offers. You would be crazy not to. I wish…"

"You wish I wasn't so smart?" Giselle teased.

"Yeah." Kurt scowled.

In a way, she understood what he was saying. He had asked her a year ago if she was serious about tracks because he didn't want to waste time coaching her, but she had given him an emphatic, 'Yes.'

No athlete was more serious than she was about tracks and especially her pet event the four-hundred-meter hurdles.

Kurt had been skeptical, but he had become her coach, and they had gotten some good results. She had medaled in a few international events.

"I was almost sure I had another 400-meter hurdles champion on my hands. We were this close." He pinched his fingers together. "This close. We would go professional. I could bask in your limelight. Train some other high paying stars… make a couple of millions…we'd get married have a couple of high performing children. I would train them too and ride the gravy train into retirement."

Giselle laughed. "Kurt, you say that to all the girls."

"No," Kurt said seriously, "just you. We shouldn't have broken up."

"But we did. Talking about it is like beating a dead dog." Giselle sighed and got up. "I am going home."

"Wait!" Kurt got up too. "You said that you weren't feeling well. Don't you want to check it out with the school doctor."

"No." Giselle shook her head. "I think my issue is lack of rest. I need some, and I need it badly. I am going to ask Pete to pick me up. He could give me a lift home. Tiana borrowed my car this morning."

Giselle pulled out her phone to text Pete. He was just across the street at the university. She knew he had evening classes.

Can I get a lift? T has my car. She texted.

"Peter Wiley," Kurt sneered, "I don't know what you see in that boy."

"He is not a boy," Giselle growled. "If you saw him recently, you wouldn't say that, and he is doing classes at the university now."

"A college freshman." Kurt snorted. "You left me for a college freshman."

"We didn't break up because of Pete," Giselle said crossly. "I told you before he is not up for discussion. I don't care who you see since we broke up."

"That's because I haven't been in a relationship with anyone," Kurt growled. "I don't spend all my waking moments trying to rob the cradle."

Giselle giggled. "You are three years older than I am, were you robbing the cradle when we were dating?"

Kurt glared at her. "I think this Pete person is bad news. He is distracting. He is young, and he is a college freshman. You just graduated from college. You have ivy league scholarships. You won a bronze medal at the CARIFTA games. You are too good for him."

Giselle glanced at her phone when it pinged. In the parking lot.

She could see Pete's black SUV through the chain link fence that separated the training area, from the parking lot.

He was sitting with the window down. He was probably waiting for Giselle to finish training. It had slipped her mind that she had told him that Tiana was going to have her car all day.

Her eyes softened at the sight of him. He was thoughtful as usual. Pete was mature beyond his years and more in tuned to her needs than anyone else.

Kurt followed closely behind her. "Oh, there is lover boy, and I do mean it literally. He is a boy, and he was spying on you. Probably insecure and jealous about us."

"Shut up, Kurt," Giselle growled. "Stop it, Pete is not up for discussion."

"You aren't sleeping with him, are you Gis?" Kurt asked suspiciously. "Is he the reason that you suddenly aren't focused on training?"

Giselle stopped walking and said as forcefully as she could. "That is none of your business!"

Kurt said just as fiercely. "You are my most promising athlete. It worries me when you are not focused!"

"I will be fine." Giselle turned toward the gate. "My life will unfold the way it is supposed to unfold."

Kurt glanced across at the parking lot again. Pete had exited the vehicle and was walking toward them. Kurt understood what Giselle was talking about. He didn't look like a boy. He had come into his own. He was leanly muscular, tall, handsome, and he knew it. He was walking like a man who knew his worth.

The girls playing netball on the other side of the parking lot had stopped training and were cat calling him. "Hey, handsome!"

"So repugnant," Kurt muttered. "Somebody needs to speak to those women about their harassment."

Giselle grinned. "Bye, Kurt. Stop worrying. I promise I will be fine by tomorrow."

****

"I don't have to ask how you are." Pete glanced at Giselle. "You look beat."

"I am." Giselle slid into the car seat and sighed. "I feel

washed out like somebody put me through a wringer."

"So we head straight to your place then?" Pete asked, he rested his hand on the steering wheel. "Too bad, I wanted to show you the progress on my house."

"I can't believe you are building a house; this is kind of surreal, you know that?" Giselle settled in her seat."

"Yes, but I am not like most teenagers." Pete grinned. "You know that."

"Only too well," Giselle murmured. "I still marvel that Preston is willing to let you live on your own."

"My dad was completely cool with it." Pete chuckled. "It was my mom that felt offended that I wanted to leave home, and she hated that it was in the same townhouse complex where you live."

"Yup, Sheryl loathes me," Giselle said forlornly, "I corrupted her innocent son."

"Giselle the corrupter," Pete grinned. "It's funny, you don't look like a corrupter now."

"How do I look?" Giselle turned to watch him lazily.

"Like I shouldn't call or text you for the evening after I drop you off, because you'll be sleeping."

"Something like that." Giselle closed her eyes. "Definitely that."

"And I shouldn't tell you congratulations about the two scholarships?" Pete asked, wryly. "I know how you get about these things."

"Who told you?" Giselle grunted." I thought it was top secret."

"We go to the same school." Pete grinned. "Whatever you do is big news. You are the Giselle Pryce, track sensation, part-time model, part-time nerd with the perfect GPA."

"I wear my sponsor's shoes!" Giselle groaned. "When did I become a model?"

"Nobody was looking at your shoes." Pete grinned his even teeth flashing in the half dark. "Anyway, congratulations."

"Thank you." Giselle nodded. "I wish I felt more upbeat about it, but at the back of my head there is this premonition, this sense of impending doom. I haven't been able to rustle up even the semblance of joy. Maybe I will after tonight."

Pete looked pensive. He glanced at her several times before finally saying what was on his mind. "Six weeks ago the condom broke, Giselle, and we got caught up in the moment after that. Maybe you are…"

"No. Giselle sat up in the seat, her weariness miraculously vanishing, "don't say it out loud. Do not send that word out in the universe. Don't jinx me."

"You have a Biology degree. You are going to do Medicine. You cannot bury your head in the sand," Pete said in exasperation. "We should be adults about this, saying the word pregnant will not make you pregnant. However, failed birth control will make you pregnant."

"Nope. I am an adult; you are barely one, and you just said it. It's out there now."

Pete laughed without mirth. He slowed down at the Wiley Complex and put his indicator on.

"What are you doing?" Giselle asked panicked.

"I am going to get a pregnancy test. Maybe two or three," Pete said, determinedly. "You are going to take it and put me out of this suspense."

"I am not pregnant." Giselle squealed, "and you are not going to go into a complex that all of your family works and buy me a pregnancy test."

She slumped in her seat when Pete ignored her.

"Pete, please." Giselle breathed, real panic taking her over. "My friend Georgia works in the pharmacy."

This was her worst nightmare coming through. She had

thought she could bury her head in the sand, and everything would come back to rights.

Her period was one week late. This was not happening. It was a glitch it would soon be back.

Her sudden tiredness and lethargy—all of it could be explained away.

She heard the alarm bells ringing, and she was ignoring them. After all, how could she be pregnant, she had taken the morning after pill.

Why was Pete forcing her to panic about this?

She almost made her way to the floor of the car and covered her head with the knapsack that she had carried with her to training.

"Pete, no!" She whispered. "Don't do this to me."

He didn't make a sound. The car door did not open. She couldn't even hear him breathe. She slowly looked up from under the bag.

Pete was staring at her and shaking his head. "Remind me which one of us is barely an adult again?"

"Oh, shut up." Giselle raged, dragging the bag back over her head.

"I guess since there is no sand to bury your head in, the bag will do." Pete sighed. "Unfortunately, I think it is better to know now. It's always better to know."

"I think this is crazy," Giselle inhaled raggedly, "I took the morning after pill. It is 95% effective."

"And then there is the pesky five percent." Pete drummed his hand on the steering wheel. "We could be in that five percent."

"No, we are not," Giselle murmured. "I don't even like kids. I don't want to be a mother! At least not now. I have school plans and track plans. This is not right. It can't be happening."

Pete sighed and then got out of the car. "I'll be back soon. Try to calm down. Fortunately for you, I like kids, and all my plans revolve around you."

Giselle closed her eyes tightly. She tried to calm down, but the very word 'pregnant' was giving her an anxiety attack.

Her life was finally going on the right trajectory. She had sacrificed a lot to be where she was now, personal relationships, sleep, delicious foods. She didn't date. She didn't party. She was the girl who got up at four o'clock in the mornings to train and then study.

And then six weeks ago it happened. It was only a matter of time before it did.

*****

She and Pete had been fooling around for months, but never going all the way.

Her defenses were down. Way down. It may have been the night. It had been perfect. She had been to a lot of receptions, but Case's had seemed almost magical. The reception had been at the back of his villa. In the gardens.

Pete had found her sitting at the sea wall, sipping her virgin daiquiri and listening to the band. He had just finished his set after serenading the couple.

"I need a shower." Pete panted, he untied his bow tie and left it hanging askew around his neck. His shirt was plastered to his back. He removed his jacket and started unbuttoning his shirt.

"What are you doing a striptease?" Giselle laughed.

"Nah, I am in IT, not the entertainment industry, and if I were to suddenly change, it would not be in front of my family. My grandmother is over there. I can't scandalize her. She is a very sweet woman. Even though if I did become a stripper, I have a feeling it would not faze her one bit."

Giselle looked to where he pointed to Pamela Santiago formerly Pamela Stone. She was the Wiley brothers' former housekeeper and Pete's grandmother. She was in a jovial conversation with her daughter Sheryl.

"I talked with her earlier. She is so in awe of her handsome, genius grandson. She even suggested to me that I should check you out."

Pete grinned. "I did show her how to change her ring tone, I guess I do qualify for the genius tag. I'll have to talk to her about trying to set me up though. I don't want a matchmaking granny."

Giselle laughed. "She said people always remark how much you look like Preston and Jordan, but she knew Joseph Wiley and you are a dead ringer of him. She called you a special type of handsome. The kind of handsome that women kill for."

Pete frowned. "Maybe she is having one too many laced drinks."

Giselle giggled. "She also said I look just like Hannah Kennedy, my aunt. And you know the Joseph and Hannah story, your grandfather, my aunt, lovers for life."

"I was looking at some pictures last night, she is right." Pete inhaled, "We do look eerily like Joseph and Hannah."

"Anyway, I need a lift tonight," Giselle said. "Both my sisters are going back to Kingston. They have work tomorrow, but I am going with you. I am looking forward to hanging with you for a while. You can tell me what I missed while I was away in Europe."

"You missed nothing." Pete snagged a drink from a passing waiter and downed it in three gulps. "I need water. Don't move. I am going to get some; I feel like I am on fire."

He came back shortly with a liter bottle half empty. "This

place is hot."

Giselle laughed. "You were on stage singing and dancing around, what do you expect?"

Pete sat beside her. "So, do you want to get out of here? My stuff is at Spring Street. I am going to have a long, long, shower."

"Why Spring Street?" Giselle raised her eyebrows, "did your parents kick you out of their villa?"

"No," Pete grinned, "I volunteered to stay at Spring Street because their villa was packed to the rafters. It's just four bedrooms. I didn't want to bunk with anyone when I could have a room of my own at Spring Street. Not that there was any less packed, but it was a first come, first serve basis. We dubbed it Stragglers Rest. Most of the band bunked there. It was a night filled with noise."

"We stayed at Guy and Lucia's place, with aunt Sharla's family."

Pete looked at her solemnly. "What if I told you I had no plans to drive back tonight. I was going to just go to Spring Street and crash and leave in the morning. Thankfully, the band won't be around tonight. I can finally get some sleep."

"Well, no problem." Giselle shrugged. "I'll stay there tonight as well."

"We, ah," Pete rubbed his face, "Gis, we'd be alone."

"I know," Giselle frowned at him, "it is a whole house. There is nothing wrong if we stay there together."

"Are you sure about that?" Pete asked intently. "Before summer we were on the verge…"

"On the verge, just the verge," Giselle smiled. "You are seriously cute, when you are serious, you know that?"

"And you are and will always be the prettiest girl in the world." Pete got up, "Let's go. I feel like I'll see steam if I step under water now."

The house on Spring Street held a morbid fascination for her. Giselle had to admit she had never stayed there overnight. She had always felt a certain revulsion to the place. After all, it was the site where her mother died, the place that had robbed her of the most important person in her life.

It was also a treasure trove of history, her mother's history, her aunt Hannah's history. She headed for the albums while Pete took his shower.

Flipping through the photos of Hannah Kennedy, Joseph Wiley and their three boys—Jordan, Guy and Case, they seemed to be such a happy family unit in the photo that it brought a smile to her face.

She paused at the pictures of her aunts Sharla and Hannah with her mom, Monique when they were young women. She slowly went through those. Putting one aside. She wanted to take that one with her.

There were a couple of pictures with her and her sisters as toddlers, they had looked identical at that age. In every picture they were dressed in the same outfits. Three of everything. One picture was even labeled—the triplets.

The more she looked at the pictures, the more nostalgic she felt. She saw one picture that was especially poignant, her mother's wedding. She was flanked by Hannah and Joseph.

Her mother looked beautiful, with a simple circle of flowers around her hair. Hannah and Joseph were both leaning in to kiss her on the cheeks.

She had the insane urge to cry which was stupid. These people have been dead for ages now and she couldn't remember any of them.

"Hey," Pete said softly, "you've been staring at that picture for minutes, what is it?"

She looked up. "I can't believe I didn't hear you."

She flipped the picture around and showed it to him. "My

mom's wedding."

"Joseph has a beard," Pete swiped his hand over his chin. "I have been contemplating trying one just like that."

Giselle laughed. "There is no need to try it, that's how yours would look."

"Look at that one," Pete pointed to another photo behind the wedding photograph. It was one of him and a pregnant Hannah. "I like that beard and moustache combo. He really was a handsome man, wasn't he?"

"Oh yes." Giselle chuckled. "And it's quite vain of you to say that."

"Look at how he looks at her. He must have loved her deeply," Pete mused, "Maybe we are them reincarnated because God knows from the moment I saw you, I loved you too. It was like I knew you were the one for me. And I was just twelve years old."

"Stop," Giselle murmured. "I don't want the kind of love these two had. He was married to another woman while she was waiting on the side. Bleh, not for me."

"The circumstances called for it." Pete shrugged. "He didn't marry for love, he married for money."

"You wouldn't dare marry another woman and have me waiting," Giselle growled. "You wouldn't be crazy!"

Pete laughed. "No, I wouldn't. Not in a million years. Besides, there would be no need to do what Joseph did; he was poor and had nothing."

"I say he should have let her try." Giselle countered. "If I were Hannah, I'd let the chips fall where they may because I would not stand for it. Not me."

"I would never ask you to." Pete had dragged her out of the chair and hugged her close. "Marry me so that we, the look-alikes, can give them a better story."

"No." Giselle had whispered. "You are crazy. I am not

getting married until I am at least thirty-five."

Pete laughed. "You have your life planned up to thirty-five?"

"Oh yes," Giselle nodded, settling in his embrace, he smelled so good and fresh. Almost minty. "I love your soap."

"I hate your answer," Pete murmured near her ears. "I am not waiting nearly twenty years for you to make a commitment. I don't feel comfortable just being your boyfriend. I want you to be tied to me forever."

"You are not my boyfriend." Giselle had replied tremulously as Pete ran his tongue lightly across her neck.

"We are not in a relationship."

"That's true," Pete slowly unzipped her dress. "We are just friends with benefits. How far are we going with this, Gis?"

Giselle jolted out of the memory and swallowed. They had gone very far. Many times. And she had not cared about consequences or her plans.

It hadn't even been a one-off. They had picked up where they left off at Spring Street. Spending most of their times together at her townhouse. Not caring about the world or consequences.

It had well and truly caught up with them now.

Chapter Two

Pete came back into the car with a paper bag in hand and two containers with food. He looked at her incredulously.

"I stopped at Yum Yum. I got your favorites. I figured you could eat. You have not moved since I left the car."

"No," Giselle murmured. "And I will not move until you drive out from this place. Your family is everywhere. Did Georgia see you at the pharmacy?"

"Yes," Pete grinned. "She said to tell you to call her. You two are due for a meet up, and she is mad at you for missing out on Nyla's birthday. Your goddaughter is one."

Giselle groaned. "Did she see you with the pregnancy test?"

"No." Pete started the car. "She was too busy being mad at you for being an absentee friend. You can get up now," Pete chuckled. "I have cleared the family den."

Giselle sat down properly in her seat and pulled on her seat belt. "When she got pregnant for Calvin, I called her foolish…told her she was throwing her future away. I also told her that it could never happen to me because I was too wise for all of this."

Pete glanced at her. "The only way you can say something like that is if you weren't having sex."

"I wasn't at the time." Giselle grimaced. "I was self-righteous and more sanctimonious than a nun. And now I am a hypocrite. I can't be pregnant though. I am too smart for this.

Pete touched her on the leg and squeezed. "You'll be fine. You know what your problem is?" Pete drove up into her townhouse complex. "You are hungry, and you are not thinking straight. We need to get some food into you, and then we deal with this."

"I am not hungry." Giselle sniffed. "I don't think I can eat a thing."

She got out of the car slowly. Pete watched her.

"Do you need help?"

"No, I am fine. Peachy," Giselle mumbled and then threw him a look of apology. "Ignore me."

Pete nodded. "Unfortunately, I am quite acquainted with your rare bouts of bad temper. I will never ignore you. It's just hard to do. He took her backpack from her and kissed her on the forehead."

Giselle smiled up at him, wanly and leaned into him. He smelled so good, a faint hint of earthy vanilla and something else. She took deep whiffs of him.

A car went slowly by her townhouse door, and she burrowed her nose even deeper into his shirt.

Why did everything feel right when she was with Pete? He clutched her to him and kissed her in her hair.

They stood on her doorstep, wordlessly for what felt like minutes. She finally stepped out of his arms and opened the door.

All the townhouses were two stories. Her bedroom and bathroom were upstairs. It had a large living room and a spacious kitchen with an island downstairs.

There was also a laundry, a half bathroom and an enclosed sunken patio which opened up to a garden.

It was a spacious two-and-a-half-bedroom townhouse. She used the half bedroom as her study.

The place was just two minutes from the Wiley Complex. It was a Wiley project spearheaded by Jordan and Shawn, and a work in progress. Ten of the townhouses were already done, another ten were still being built. One of those was Pete's. He checked it every time he visited her.

"I am going to get a shower," she said over her shoulder to Pete.

"Okay. I'll wait until you are done before I start eating." He headed for the home entertainment system and turned on the radio.

She looked at him and wondered what he was thinking, feeling. So far in her panicked state, she was thinking all about herself. Pete was as usual inscrutable.

He looked at her lazily. "The food will get cold if you don't hurry."

Giselle headed upstairs. "I'll be down before you know it."

"Maybe you should take these with you." Pete held up the paper bag with the pregnancy tests.

Giselle walked back down the stairs as if weights were around her legs and inhaled raggedly. "I guess this is it."

Pete nodded. "And I am here…always, okay."

"Okay." She took the package and slowly made her way up the stairs to the sounds of Peter Lloyd's cover of John Lennon's Woman.

She had the thing on repeat. That particular song, Woman,

brought back memories. She wondered if Pete remembered that he sang that song to her.

She paused and came back down the stairs to ask him. He had his eyes closed and was singing softly to the song. Woman I know you understand the little child within your man, please remember my life is in your hands...

Her eyes teared up, and she headed back upstairs. That was the song, the one that brought her partially out of denial about him.

She headed toward the shower; her head full of memories.

****

Summer 2012

"Your Aunt Sharla is on my case again!" Toddy said as soon as Giselle stepped into the house. Tiana and Elsa followed close behind. She wants the three of you for the summer.

"Cool." Giselle nodded happily. She loved her aunt Sharla, and usually spent holidays with her.

"Not cool. She is coming out here this time." Toddy grumbled. "Apparently, most of your Wiley cousins are getting married, Saint, Preston, Jordan. It makes sense for her to be out here now."

"She is going to find out that Celine left me. I can't have her thinking that you are motherless and that I am a philanderer who can't keep a wife."

"But we are motherless." Giselle rolled her eyes. "And you are a philanderer who can't keep a wife."

Tiana snickered. "Remember Brandy? She was what, wife number two? She was here all of two years. I can barely remember her."

"And then there was Carmelita." Elsa chuckled.

"She wasn't a wife." Giselle shook her head. "Just a girlfriend. I liked aunty Celine though, she was really nice."

"Couldn't stand her son, Mason Magnus. Stuck up doesn't begin to describe him." Elsa smirked, "When she had him over the little twerp used to sit and stare at me unblinkingly behind his thick glasses."

"Oh, stop it, Mason was a good boy." Toddy sighed. "Very quiet and mousy. A sensitive sort, we had no connection really. Unfortunately, he blames me for the breakup, which technically wasn't true. I didn't want to break up with Celine. She was my one great love. She was supposed to have been the last wife."

"She caught you cheating," Elsa said disapprovingly. "You need adult supervision. People get it wrong; we are your guardians, not the other way around. If you didn't have us, who knew what you would get up to."

Toddy laughed. A deep belly chuckle. "There might be some truth in that."

Giselle looked at him dispassionately. He was an attractive man. He looked a lot like their father and the men in the Pryce family. He was tall, broad-shouldered. He had a straight as an arrow nose, over generous lips, high cheekbones, coffee dark skin, and light brown eyes. It was a striking combination.

He kept his hair low to hide his greys, and he ate well and exercised. Nobody would guess that Jonathan Theodore Pryce, affectionately called Toddy was sixty-two.

Old women, young women, middle-aged women chased him like it was sport. Added to that, he was senator, owned an advertising firm that was profitable and was extremely generous with his women friends. Maybe too generous, Celine had taken him to the cleaners recently, or that was what Toddy said.

They lived in a seven-bedroom house in the exclusive

Smokey Vale area. It had a breathtaking view of the city, but it was too big for the four of them. They had two housekeepers, one of them, Myrna was a live-in housekeeper and was more their mother than any of the women that Toddy paraded in and out of their lives.

They hardly saw Toddy; he was too busy for domestic life, but they did get to see him more than his children and grandchildren.

Toddy made an effort with them. He often said, he did it for their father Wilton Pryce who died before they were born.

Theirs was not the traditional nuclear family unit, but it worked. At least it had for the last thirteen years. Toddy had taken them as toddlers to live with himself and his wife at the time, Brandy. She hadn't stuck around for long. After she had left, they had gone through a spate of nannies. It seemed as if the nannies usually fell for Toddy and then quit or were fired after the relationships inevitably went south.

Myrna was the only woman it seemed who was immune to Toddy Pryce. She was fifty years old, and she couldn't be charmed by Toddy. He treated her with the deference of a valued employee, and she ran the household like it was her own. She was the stabilizing force in the house. Giselle suspected that it was because of Myrna and her steadying presence that Toddy was not particularly committed to any of his partners. He knew his domestic life was being run smoothly. He didn't need a wife for that.

"Girls!" Myrna called before they headed upstairs to their individual rooms.

They stopped. Elsa almost colliding with Tiana.

"Your cousin Jordan is inviting you to a party. It is an adoption party or something like that. You have a new family member, Peter Wiley."

"He is not our family. He is Preston's son." Giselle pointed out. "We are not related to Preston."

"I keep forgetting." Myrna shrugged. "Anyway, he is officially adopted, and you are all invited to this party to meet him."

"Sounds boring." Tiana scoffed.

"I have stuff to do," Elsa muttered. "I am tired of meeting new family members."

"You are all going." Toddy bellowed. "I won't have Jordan and Guy accuse me of keeping you three from the Wiley family. I hate butting heads with that side of your family."

"But Toddy…" Giselle groaned; she hadn't even gotten the chance to find an excuse.

"No buts." Toddy pointed at them. "I don't want Jordan telling Sharla that I am not accommodative to that side of the family. It's just a party. If they want you to meet a new member of the family, you'll do it."

"This Pete boy is not family!" Giselle complained. "I wanted to go to the movies."

"You are going to the party!" Toddy leveled her with his fiercest scowl and then walked toward his office.

****

"What does one wear to an adoption party?" Giselle looked in her cavernous closet at all the clothes she had in there and worried her lip.

There was a knock on her door, and she yelled for whoever to come in. It was Tiana. She had the same question.

Giselle looked at her in the mirror. "Just do not wear anything like what I am wearing."

"As if," Tiana snorted and sat on the bed. "You dress like a boy. And Elsa dresses like a hippie. Unfortunately, I am the only one who knows fashion."

Giselle chuckled. Tiana was right. She knew fashion and makeup and all of that stuff. She spent hours in the mirror getting the right shades and things right. She had even modeled for one of Toddy's girlfriend's clothing brand last summer.

Giselle withdrew a jeans and a red halter top blouse from the closet and held it up. "This is what I am wearing."

Tiana made a face. "Why not try a dress? That black and white dress is pretty."

"No." Giselle shook her head. "I am wearing this."

"Well, I like that dress." Tiana headed for the dress. "It is nice. Where did you get it?"

"Aunt Sharla." Giselle shrugged. "She probably meant to give it to me. Tiana took the dress from the hanger and plastered it to herself. It is definitely me."

Giselle giggled. "Okay. You can have it."

"Thank you," Tiana grinned at her in the mirror. "You are my bestest sister. You are generous and kind and…"

"Get out of my room," Giselle chuckled. "Leave. You won't even have space to put that dress when you are done wearing it. You have so many clothes already."

"How are you wearing your hair?" Tiana looked at her in horror. "Not in that ponytail? Why can't you change up your style for a while?"

"Not happening." Giselle nodded. "It's a kids party, not a fashion show."

"You always wear the same style," Tiana said in despair. "I wish you would let me help you with it. You should cut it, put some layers in there, give it a highlight."

"Help Elsa with hers," Giselle said, knowing full well that Elsa would not have Tiana anywhere near her hair or her closet. Elsa had a definite way that she liked to do things, and nobody could sway her to do otherwise. In that regard, they were very much alike, personality wise they were vastly different.

They resembled quite a bit, but they were not identical. They had the same honey brown skin, more or less, Tiana had the lightest complexion of the three. They both had the Pryce nose, it was straight as an arrow and flared at the end, just like Toddy's. They had the same almond-shaped eyes, another Pryce inheritance. People always commented that they had a little Asian in them, especially when they were younger. They had different shades of brown eyes. Giselle's was medium brown, the same shade as coconut sugar. Elsa had made the observance years ago and had nicknamed her Coco Sugs because of her eyes. Thank God the nickname hadn't caught on. She preferred, good old Giselle or Gis.

Elsa's eyes were dark, almost black, and Tiana had light whiskey-colored eyes, just like the Pryce's.

Giselle and Elsa looked like their aunt Hannah, Jordan, Guy and Case Wiley's mother.

Her aunt Sharla said it every time she saw them, and it was obvious in pictures.

Giselle looked more like Hannah these days because she kept her hair long. She had never cut it. Her long thick jet-black corkscrew curls hung to her hips in a fat thick plait. Elsa, on the other hand, hated long hair. She kept it short and sometimes shaved the sides. At other times she dyed it blond or red or whatever color she felt like.

Tiana had a lighter complexion than them. Her hair was more wavy than curly, and it was dark brown, not black.

Elsa came in when Tiana was on the way out. She was already dressed in her favorite color of the month, lavender. She was in a bohemian blouse top with double ruffles on the sleeve and jeans shorts. Elsa had six piercings in her left ear and only one in her right.

She had gotten them despite the protests from both Sharla and Toddy. She even had a tattoo on her lower back of her first and second name, Elsa Cara. Toddy had discovered that she had it when they went to a pool party for one of his friends. He had almost blown a fuse. He claimed that Elsa was out to kill him.

If there was a spectrum, she was on the conservative side, and Elsa was extremely liberal. In Giselle's eyes, Elsa was the most interesting one of the three of them. There was something reckless and non-conformist about Elsa. Giselle feared it and disapproved of it and envied it all at the same time.

She sometimes wished she wasn't as dogged, and one-track minded in her pursuits. She would do well with some Elsa like qualities sprinkled in with the straight and narrow path she had chosen for herself.

"What do you think we would be like if Jennifer Riddley Wiley hadn't killed our mother and aunt?" Giselle wondered out loud. "Would I be the same stick in the mud kind of person that I am now?"

Elsa made herself comfortable on the bed and yawned.

"I doubt that. We wouldn't be the same," Elsa said lazily. "We would have grown up with our real mother. The sweetest dearest woman on the planet according to aunt Sharla. You and Tiana would not be so, I don't know how to put this nicely, damaged."

"Damaged?" Giselle laughed. "And why are you excluded?"

Elsa chuckled. "I am fine despite the odds. I am like Peter Wiley, bad odds, but I turned out fine. Did you hear his story? He escaped from an orphanage. Escaped! And then he walked from one end of the island to the other. And he survived. He is tough."

"I wonder about that," Giselle mused. "Do you think he is really Preston's child? And how on earth did he happen to grow up in the foster care system, the Wiley's are rich."

"The boy is definitely a Wiley." Elsa nodded. "I saw him when I went to hang with Guy over at the farm. He looks just like Preston. He is going to be seriously cute when he gets older. And Guy said Sheryl was not mentally stable when she gave him up for adoption. She was in an accident or something."

"They had him when they were fifteen." Giselle shook her head, "our age. Toddy would blow a fuse if that happened to any of us."

"That's why I am staying away from penises like the plague," Elsa murmured. "Stupid Toddy thinks I am going to be the first one of us to get pregnant. He threatens me about it every day. I don't understand why," Elsa said innocently. "It's Tiana who has the gigantic crush on the cute new teacher at school. You know she writes her English essays about the two of them. Have you read her stories?"

"No," Giselle giggled.

"They are so hot. I showed one to Myrna, and she started to fan. I then showed her a picture of James Dalton, and she said she understood why Tianna is losing her head."

"He is cute." Giselle grinned, "he is all Georgia talks about at school since he started teaching there. She even signed up for his extra classes, and she has training. I am yet to see how she will juggle the two."

"I heard James Dalton," Tiana came back into the room. "What are you saying about him?"

"Georgia likes him too," Giselle grinned, "you have competition."

Tiana groaned. "None of us stand a chance. He has a fiancé, whom he loves to death and we are underage girls who have no self-control and will get a person in trouble. He told me that he doesn't encourage the attention of bratty teenagers."

"How would you know all that?" Giselle asked.

"Because I showed him one of my… er… stories." Tiana turned toward the door. "I used different names and all. I wanted to impress him with my writing. I have no idea why he would assume that the characters are about him and me."

"Maybe because you call the guy Wames Walton and the girl Giana Bryce. It doesn't take a genius, Tiana." Elsa smirked. "James and Wames and Giana and Tiana…"

Tiana shrugged. "He gave me a low score for my efforts. And basically said it sucked. Personally, I thought the story was so good. Now, I am not sure if I still love him or hate him."

Elsa grinned. "It was a bit too steamy, bordering on porn. I showed it to Myrna, and she drank some water when she reached the second page. And it was just the second page. It had ten pages. Quite an essay."

"Oh, for the love of God!" Tiana squealed. "Why did you show it to Myrna?"

"Because you told stupid Mason Magnus that I love him and since then he has been looking at me strangely. He is a weird man," Elsa said gleefully. "I am personally happy that the bug-eyed twerp no longer has a reason to drop by the house since his mother is no longer here."

"He is not bug-eyed. It's his glasses!" Giselle said, "it gives him that effect. Mason is a very nice person, Elsa."

"No, he is not." Elsa pouted. "He is strange. He hardly speaks. He just sits and observes like he is practicing to be the wallpaper in a play."

Giselle shook her head. "You two are crazy!"

"Nah, we are normal." Elsa pointed at her, "you are the crazy one. You are little Miss Perfect with your perfect grades in the Sciences and dedication to tracks. Everybody knows that athletes are not great students simply because training is so taxing, but no, not you. You have taken it up a notch. If you keep up this pace you won't have a life when you are older."

"Yep," Tiana nodded. "She is obsessed with Toddy's praise. I can't even get a B around here without being compared to Superwoman Giselle."

Giselle smiled. "I am a hundred percent focused. If you two applied yourself a little bit more..."

"Ha," Elsa snorted. "I only have one life; I intend to stop and smell the roses. Have fun. Embrace my imperfections. Live!"

"Oh shut it," Giselle threw a pillow at her and then at Tiana who was making a face. "The two of you are jealous."

"You know what she needs?" Tiana said ominously. "A boy to derail her. A handsome prince to mess with her focus, so that she can start getting Bs."

"Not going to happen," Giselle said happily. "I am immune to love and crushes and all of that teenage girl nonsense. I have one goal in mind, well two...I am going to be an Olympic and World Championship Gold medalist, and I will show up in the history books as breaking some records, and I am going to be a doctor, specializing in Sports Medicine."

****

The party was by the poolside. Giselle loved visiting the Wiley Complex. The houses were the right size, not the cavernous monstrosity she had grown up in, and they had a recreational and pool area that reminded her of a four-star hotel without the crowds.

Jordan was the first one to greet them when they left the

car. He spoke to Toddy's driver briefly, telling him that he would drop them home when it was time, and then he turned to them.

"Cousins!"

Jordan hugged Tiana and Elsa first, and then he turned to her.

"Gis, my love!"

"Jordan, my love." She grinned at him and then hugged him tightly. He had been away in Dubai for two years.

"I missed you," she murmured in his neck, "don't go away so long again."

"I won't." Jordan squeezed her to him. "I am thinking of staying here. Listen for a wedding invite. Don't breathe a word of it to Shawn. It is a secret."

"A secret wedding for you and Shawn?" Giselle asked solemnly.

"That's right. So top secret we can't talk about it now. Shawn doesn't know."

"You are weird," Giselle whispered. "How can a woman get married without knowing. It's impossible."

"It will be the surprise of the century." Jordan chuckled. "She loves surprises, she'll get it. Oh, she'll get it."

Tiana and Elsa were involved in greeting the other cousins. They knew to give her and Jordan time alone. They had a close bond. Closer than he had with the other girls.

Jordan thought she reminded him the most of his mother.

Jordan laughed. "Shawn is the weird one, I have to adjust to her weirdness. Have you met Pete?"

"No." Giselle shook her head. "Is this going to be a large party?"

Jordan shook his head. "Just family. I wanted Pete to meet you three. You are pretty close in age."

"He is twelve years old." Giselle made a face, "not close

in age at all."

"He is going to be joining your school in September. You are going to be nice to him. I can count on you to do that."

Giselle snorted. "I am three years ahead of him. Giselle shrugged. We won't run in the same crowd."

"Still, look out for him," Jordan said sternly. "He is family."

"Your family." Giselle pouted. "But I'll look out for him. Besides, I don't think he will need looking out for. Bellfield is an exclusive school. If he is a small wimpy kid that is the best place to send him. They frown on bullying."

Jordan laughed. "Small, wimpy kid? You really need to meet him. Pete!"

He turned to the pool area and called.

Giselle didn't know what she was expecting. Maybe it was a smaller boy with braces and a limp, but she wasn't expecting that he would look older than twelve or that he would be on the same height as her or that he would be so good looking. Elsa was right, he looked just like Preston and Elsa was wrong; he didn't need a couple of years to be super cute.

He walked toward them a self-assured smirk on his face. "What's up, uncle Jordan?"

"This is Giselle," Jordan said to Pete. "My cousin."

Pete smiled at her. "Hi Giselle."

Giselle swallowed. She felt uneasy just staring at him. It was the strangest sensation. She never felt that way when she looked at Preston, and this was a younger version of him, down to the mole on his neck.

"Hey." She smiled hardly able to meet his eyes.

"I think you can see that Pete is not er small," Jordan said quite oblivious to the tension between them.

Giselle nodded.

Pete was staring at her intently, his hand was in his pockets, and he appeared relaxed, but he wasn't.

She was happy when Tiana and Elsa joined them, and she could escape Pete.

It was his party, but something about him unsettled her.

Chapter Three

They never had a proper conversation until Jordan's wedding to Shawn. Pete was the one who sang the bridal song. It was the first time she was hearing him sing, and she was blown away.

He could sing. Really sing. And he was in high demand after the service. Everybody wanted to gush over him. It was understandable. He was the main attraction for the family who had not heard his story or met him yet.

The afternoon was beautiful, slightly overcast, cool, and breezy. It was quite perfect in the hills of Irish Town. She looked around for Tiana who had her camera, but she was somewhere in the crush of people.

Elsa was laughing and chatting with Shawn's sister Athena. They were good friends. Whenever they spent the summer in Florida, with Sharla, Athena would take Elsa under her wings. They were having a giggle fest over something or the other. Giselle didn't want to intrude.

She looked in the crowd and realized that she didn't have anyone to hang with. She was not like her socialite sisters. She hated small talk.

She wandered down to the infinity poolside and sat down, arranging her aqua blue knee-length dress around her. Sharla had insisted that she wear the dress with a matching headband. Her hair was out, and as usual, she had to take care that she didn't sit on it.

Her sisters thought she was ridiculous for keeping her hair this long, but she liked it. Her mother had kept her hair long. It was something that they had in common. The only tenuous bond she had in her mind for a woman who was long dead.

"You look like a mermaid," Pete sat beside her, "a sad mermaid. You should look happier, it's a wedding."

She grinned at him. She couldn't help it. He looked adorable in his tux but then again, adorable was too tame a word. She had uncomfortable feelings for Pete Wiley. In the past weeks since his adoption party, she had dismissed it as an anomaly. He was just twelve. She was fifteen. She would not put these feelings into context or acknowledge them.

"You sounded good today." She sat up straighter. "I love that John Legend song, Stay With You."

Pete nodded. "Thanks. I like it too. One day I am going to sing it to someone special."

Giselle nodded solemnly. "She will be one lucky lady if you genuinely mean the words."

He smiled.

And she almost gasped. How was it that his teeth were so straight and white? He should have crooked boy teeth.

And why was she constantly reminding herself that he was just a boy? She needed her head examined. She needed a boyfriend. Both Elsa and Tiana had already had boyfriends. Toddy was quite fine with them having platonic friendships with boys, they could even go on dates if they were heavily chaperoned.

Maybe she should find someone her age to be feeling uncomfortable about. Was it that easy though? She hadn't wanted to until now.

"What's wrong?" Pete asked her softly. His eyes looked concerned, and she realized that she had been staring into space and frowning.

"Nothing." Giselle shook her head. "I er was just thinking."

Pete looked at her, knowingly. And for a stark minute she thought that he could read her thoughts and then he looked away.

Twelve-year-old boys were not wise and intuitive. She was reading him wrong. He could not know that he had an effect on her. He would never know. It would pass. She would laugh about it to her sisters or her best friend Georgia.

"Is it true that you were caught stealing in the supermarket, and then you were brought to Preston, and then he realized that you were his son?" Giselle asked him, changing the subject from the inappropriate attraction she was harboring for him in her head.

Pete nodded. "I was hungry. I walked from the other end of the island for weeks. I was determined to find my grandmother Pamela Stone."

"And you found your father instead?" Giselle shook her head, "it is an unbelievable coincidence."

Pete watched as her hair rippled as she moved, he seemed mesmerized.

Giselle snapped her fingers. "Pete?"

"You are the prettiest girl I have ever seen," Pete said dazedly. "I mean, sorry."

Giselle grinned. "I can't be the prettiest girl you have ever seen. I do look like my sisters, which means they are equally as pretty."

"I know," Pete said, "but you are different."

"You were telling me about meeting your father," Giselle said a pleased smile spreading over her face. He thought she was pretty and different. Her uncomfortable feelings were not flowing in one direction.

Her elation about that should be laughable, but strangely she felt better. More confident that she was not in this madness alone.

"I hated the boys' home where I was placed after my foster mother decided to stop fostering, so I decided to find my grandmother. And so I escaped, walked all the way to Kingston. I thought my parents were dead or something, but then I found them."

"I wouldn't mind having a story like that," Giselle said wistfully. "I wish my parents were not gone forever."

Pete looked at her quizzically. "Uncle Jordan said that my grandmother killed your mother."

"Yup." Giselle nodded and then shrugged off the story. She didn't want to talk about that. It was sort of morbid to be thinking about murders at a wedding.

"I want to hear more about your journey to Kingston."

They talked way into the evening. They even went and got food together.

"I love this place," Giselle said dreamily. "I would stay here. I would do a spa treatment and then lounge on one of the balconies and watch the sunset."

"Sounds good." Pete nodded. "I'd do that too with you."

Giselle looked at him sharply. "Peter Wiley, you are too young to be so fresh."

He grinned. "I figured you were talking in the future."

"We may not even be in contact in the future," Giselle said primly. "I'll be a world-famous athlete and doctor."

"And I'll be your faithful stalker." Pete shrugged. "Trust me, we'll be in contact."

The conversation moved on to their favorite songs and movies and games. They had a lot of things in common.

It was only natural that they exchanged numbers. They still had a lot to talk about.

****

2013

Giselle and Pete drifted into something of a friendship and became each other's hang out partner at family gatherings. And there were many. Walter Wiley was a party king, and he found something to celebrate every other month, and usually, the Pryce sisters were invited.

At school, Pete was in his second year when she was a senior. He was popular, with the teachers and the students. Even her senior friends who should know better gushed over Pete.

"I think he is going to be a famous singer," Georgia murmured after they listened to Pete sing the national anthem. "My little sister is in his class, and she is determined to join his entourage before he really makes it big."

Georgia was her best friend. She and her sister Malia attended Bellfield.

The private school cost an arm and a leg because they had small classes and fancy extracurricular activities like horseback riding and archery. Stuff that regular schools did not offer.

"He doesn't want to do it professionally," Giselle said as they exited the school's auditorium, "he wants to do something in computers. Malia should plan to join someone else's entourage."

"And you would know this," Georgia said knowingly. "Because you talk to him all the time. Every day. Every night."

"We talk." Giselle shrugged. "Not every day or every night. He is cool."

"And you like him." Georgia hissed. "You like a thirteen-year-old kid. There are so many boys our age, and you like Malia's crush."

"Stop it," Giselle said without heat.

"I don't know what it is about Pete, he has the teachers fawning over him at school, Malia never shuts up about him at home and you, my best friend, you like him."

"And how would you know that?" Giselle growled. "I never talk about him. I only see him at family parties or the occasional time when I visit my cousin's farm. We have family in common. Our interaction is unavoidable."

"He has a thing for you too." Georgia looked at her knowingly, "Malia says that you are all he talks about, and he has a picture of you as his phone screen saver."

"He will outgrow it." Giselle shrugged. "That's what my aunt Sharla says about my sisters' crushes.

"Oh goodness," Giselle pointed toward the staff room, "Mr. Dalton is dressed in all black. Fan me."

Giselle elbowed her. "What's with you girls and Mr. Dalton?"

"He is foin. Foin, I tell you." Georgia squinted her eyes and looked at Giselle. "If you can't see it? You need glasses?"

"I can see he is good looking, and no, I don't need glasses." Giselle glared at Georgia. "I don't get the hype about James Dalton. You and Tiana and everyone else…"

"We are normal. Georgia giggled, "I mean who can stare upon the beauty that is Mr. James Dalton, the perfect symmetry of his face, the come hither look in his green eyes and not want to write poems? He makes me want to take English Literature so that I can have one extra class with him."

"He does nothing for me." Giselle snorted. "And I would never, not in a million years take English Literature."

"Well, then, that's one girl out of the competition." Georgia grinned, "We all know the reason why you are immune to Mr. Dalton."

"What's the reason, pray tell?" Giselle asked primly.

"Because you just have the hots for a boy. A little wittle boy in my sister's class."

And they were back to Pete.

"Pete is not a little wittle boy," Giselle defended knowing full well she was playing into Georgia's hands by protesting.

Georgia laughed. "It's true he looks older than his age, but he is still a whole three grades lower than us. Why don't you give Calvin in our class a chance? He likes you."

"He acts like a buffoon." Giselle snorted. "He is constantly boasting about who likes him. Somehow that makes him unattractive."

"What about the new trainer over at the track club?" Georgia stopped to tie her shoelace and then took a while to smooth down her khaki skirt.

Giselle waited on her impatiently. At Bellfield, they wore a uniform—green and white polo shirts and khaki bottoms, skirts for girls, and pants for boys.

"Aren't you going to answer?" Georgia glared at her. "Don't pretend that you didn't hear."

"I am guessing that you are talking about Kurt Yu?" Giselle snorted. "No, not interested."

"I like him, Georgia straightened up. "He is gorgeous. I think he looks like a model. Korean and black is a good,

good mix."

"Why don't we talk about something else? Giselle asked exasperated. "I get enough about this at home. Both my sisters think Kurt is cute."

"I am sure he likes you." Georgia sighed. "He gives you special attention."

"Maybe because I am the fastest hurdler in my class." Giselle grimaced. "Not to boast or anything but the National Sports paper said, I am one to watch."

"No, it's not the fact that you can run." Georgia shook her head. "All the boys like you and your sisters. I am so envious. I would like to spend a couple days in your shoes and experience the joys of being flawless. You are really pretty, and yet you don't act like it."

"You're envious of me? Why?" Giselle raised an eyebrow and looked at her friend whose heart-shaped face and bow lips was the definition of cute.

"Maybe it's the fact that you have a smooth blemish free complexion," Georgia mused. "It is so flawless that you look as if you don't have pores. Meanwhile, I have to hunt down the odd zit and smother it with clay before it leaves a spot."

Giselle chuckled. "Clay huh? I must remember that for my zit's because I occasionally get them. I don't exist in a movie world."

"And then there are your teeth all perfect and white. Meanwhile, I am going to be fitted with braces for the summer."

"But when you smile, you have the cutest dimples." Giselle pointed out. "And my teeth are perfect because I got braces at ten. Tiana and Elsa didn't need it. They are the ones with the perfect teeth."

Georgia smiled, flashing her dimples. "I know you had braces, but the grass is greener…"

"Thanks for the compliments Georgie but you have to be thankful for what you have. You don't want to be me in any way shape or form. You have parents that love you, a close-knit family, a mom who bakes cookies…and goes shopping with you and listens to your million and one complaints. A dad who loves his girls and is always there for them. To me, your grass is greener."

Georgia made a face. "You are right. I do have the best parents; I can't complain about that. I am sorry for being an envious toad."

"Apology accepted." Giselle gave her the side eye, "and how is a pretty girl to act? I should go around and wave to an adoring crowd expecting people to lick my boots?"

"No," Georgia giggled. "You should, you know, act more girly instead of like one of the boys. Give the cute guys some attention. Calvin is so cute, but you act like he isn't even alive. And Kurt Yu, goodness, when he walks near me my legs tremble. I don't know how you do it… act like you don't care about either one."

"Easy." Giselle made a face. "Calvin acts like an idiot. Pete is more mature than he is. And Kurt is not…"

"Pete," Georgia finished. "Pete. It all comes back to Pete."

Giselle growled. "I was going to say Kurt is not into his trainees like that. He is a professional."

"Yeah, to everyone but you." Georgia shook her head. "You just don't see it, or you don't want to see it because of Pete Wiley."

Giselle breathed a sigh of relief when they reached their classroom. "I am not interested in Kurt or Calvin or whoever and stop it about Pete, okay. He is just a friend. A young friend. A boy. Innocent."

And she intended to put an end to their close friendship. It was getting out of hand. It was feeling strange.

Georgia's eyes widened at every word she said, but she nodded vigorously. "Okay. I will not tease you about Pete again. My lips are sealed."

"You do that." Giselle couldn't help giving her a parting shot.

****

"My mom chose Life of Pi for movie night," Pete called her later that evening. "And we were discussing some of the lessons we learned."

"Tell me about it." Giselle murmured. She was bone tired. Kurt had pushed her hard this evening in anticipation of the competition later.

"You know it's better when we watch the movie together." Pete chuckled. "You always promise to watch one with me, and then I end up telling you about them, and then you end up not interested in seeing it."

"I have no time for movies young grasshopper. I have CARIFTA in a few days." Giselle closed her eyes tiredly. "Just tell me."

"Nope, this one we are going to watch together. Come over tomorrow. You don't have training tomorrow, do you?"

"Yep. I have training." Giselle exhaled. "Stevens, my main coach, is setting up a mock competition with all the trainees. Boys against girls. I can't wait."

"Can I come and see you?" Pete asked. "I'll ask uncle Jordan to take me. We can watch the movie together after."

Giselle sighed. She had determined to draw back from Pete. They were too close. Besides Georgia and her sisters, he was her main friend.

"I don't know." She hesitated. "When did we get so close? Do you realize that we spend all of my spare time together?"

"That's not a bad thing." Pete cajoled. "You like the same things I do."

"Not everything," Giselle said hesitantly. "I don't like fish, you do, and I don't like saxophone music."

Pete laughed. "I have music lessons tomorrow with Miss Curry. We are supposed to choose our instrument, and I chose the saxophone."

"Next year, choose the violin," Giselle said jokingly. "And then play me Vivaldi Four Seasons—Spring. I like that."

"Okay," Pete said seriously.

"I was joking." Giselle chuckled. "You don't have to do any such thing."

"But he did. A few months after that, Pete played Vivaldi, Four Seasons— Spring in the general assembly at school. He actually dedicated it to her with a beaming Miss Curry standing behind him like a proud parent.

"Never have I had a music prodigy such as Pete." She announced to the assembly. "I am proud to say he learned this instrument in six weeks."

"And I am dedicating this one to Giselle Pryce who won bronze at the CARIFTA games."

All the school turned to look at her before he started playing.

"Oh for the love of all that is smitten," Georgia whispered beside her. "Puppy love."

"Shut up," Giselle grunted.

"Just for his Giselle." Georgia mocked when Pete finished playing, and the whole assembly gave him a standing ovation.

"You are going to have to cut this boy loose, Gis," Georgia said when they were on their way to class.

"But why?" Giselle growled.

"Because you don't learn violin for a girl in six weeks without some serious feelings behind it."

"He is just a friend." Giselle protested.

"He doesn't think he is just a friend." Georgia warned. "There is no space in your life for him. Let him have a crush on someone else, my sister Malia for instance. You have to cut him loose, or else you will hurt him."

****

Giselle pondered the situation all day. She didn't want to cut off Pete. She liked him. A little bit too much.

"I'll help you do it," Georgia said. "He is a little boy. Don't worry he will recover, but you can't let him be so obsessed. You are doing him a favor."

Toddy's driver came for them that evening, to take them to the High-Velocity Training Center at the university. Pete came to wait with them. His mother usually picked him up.

"Hey," he said to them in his confident way. "What's up?"

"Training is up." Georgia grinned. "We have a new fabulous trainer named Kurt Yu, and he likes Gis. We can't wait to go to practice."

Giselle looked at Pete, and their eyes met. There was a shocked expression in his eyes and then the unmistakable blaze of jealousy.

Pete was not going to take this well.

Giselle inhaled raggedly; she was going to cruelly nip their friendship in the bud. It gave her a strange, painful pang.

"People like me, loads of guys like me," she said snarkily, "and Kurt is not a boy, he is nineteen, in university doing his degree in sports management. I am more attracted to that age level."

Pete nodded; his expression became unreadable. "I see."

Georgia giggled adding fuel to the fire. "Giselle is his favorite trainee. He gives her extra attention."

Pete didn't move. Giselle could feel his mind working, sense his jealousy. It gave her no joy, but she had to break whatever weirdness was between them. They were getting too close. They texted each other late into the night and called each other too often. She was three years older, it irked her that she had so much in common with a thirteen-year-old boy.

She needed to spend more time with people in her own age group.

And then her ride came, and she casually waved goodbye to Pete as she and Georgia went into the car. She couldn't help but notice that he had a little slouch to his shoulders, and he looked a bit woebegone when she went into the car. It had to be done.

****

"Let's do this." Kurt blew his whistle, and they went into the starting blocks, all seven of them. He was assisting coach Stevens. As usual, he was his no-nonsense self. Giselle had no idea where Georgia got her fanciful idea that Kurt was attracted to her. He was professional with a capital P.

She didn't do well in training that evening because she was constantly thinking about Pete's expressions. She felt as if she had kicked a puppy. The mean feeling created a tightness in her chest that would not dislodge.

Kurt pulled her aside after she had knocked down a couple of hurdles and asked her point blank. "What's eating you, Giselle?"

"Nothing." She panted. Feeling an absurd urge to cry. She didn't want to lose Pete as a friend. She was regretting her spontaneous decision to cut him down.

And it had been a cut-down. I am more attracted to that age

level. She heard her own voice playing in her head.

"Whatever it is," Kurt said urgently, "let it go. The CARIFTA games are coming up in April, you are our most promising under 17 female athlete, you have to focus."

Giselle nodded uncertainly and then said weakly. "Okay."

"You can't allow boys to get under your skin," Kurt said wryly.

"Boys which boys?" Giselle asked heatedly.

"You are a pretty girl, they chase you. Don't let it get to your head. Don't let relationships get to your head." Kurt looked at her dispassionately. "Don't waver from your goal. You can be one of the greats to come out of Jamaica. Stay focused."

Giselle made a face. The little pep talk did manage to act like a douse of cold water. Pete was just a boy; she would no doubt disappoint plenty of boys in her future. She had bigger fish to fry. Her track career was too important to be playing around with.

She vowed never to get distracted again.

Chapter Four

Giselle read the instructions and peed on the stick. She read it again and again. It said one line for no, two lines for yes. She looked at herself in the mirror. She was looking a little haggard around the edges. She should have walked away that day when Preston had met her at the door and asked her to fix her computer elsewhere. She would not be doing this.

She wouldn't have fallen for Pete, so utterly and conclusively. She wouldn't have spent months trying to suppress her feelings for him. She wouldn't have started dating Kurt Yu just because she wanted to put distance between her and Pete.

It hadn't quite worked out the way she imagined because Pete had started seeing other people too. It seemed as if every other month, he had a new girlfriend. It had made her rabidly jealous.

The test highlighted two lines. Giselle stepped into the

shower feeling dizzy. She was pregnant. She turned on the hot water and stood under there until it felt as if it were burning her skin. Her hair got wet, she ended up giving it a quick wash.

Somehow, now that she knew she wasn't feeling as panicked. She calmly bathed, inhaling and exhaling to calm herself. When she stepped out of the shower she plugged in her diffuser. She had accidentally discovered that spearmint and lime essential oils made a wonderful fragrance and she waited for it to permeate the bathroom before she took big whiffs of it while staring at the pregnancy tests like they were aliens.

She wasn't going to tell anybody about the pregnancy. She would ask Amara, one of the girls in her track club, where she went to have her abortion last year, and she would do it.

Simple.

Then she could continue her life as if this never happened. It wouldn't be her proudest moment, but nobody had to know about this. Just her and God.

God.

She closed her eyes, he would know. He made her. He could punish her for this. Every pro-life sermon was ringing in her ear like a cacophony of sounds.

It was easy to say that she was pro-life when she didn't have an unplanned pregnancy, two scholarships to choose from, and a track career that was going places.

Shut up, she whispered to the voices in her head.

She would lose her scholarships if she kept the baby or babies. Her mother had triplets naturally.

She shuddered when she thought of that. She went to the diffuser and took a couple of big whiffs of the scent. It was supposed to relax her, but it wasn't doing the job.

She leaned back on the counter.

This would set back her training for a year, and she'd eventually give up just like Georgia. Her friend had gotten pregnant in the second year of college. She had dropped out of the track program, had taken the year off, and had barely scraped through to finish her degree. Her priorities had changed.

Now she had a baby for Calvin.

Calvin was immature and had moved on before she even had the baby.

And what about her, Giselle Pryce. She was pregnant for a teenager. A freshman in college. His family would hate her. Her family would be majorly disappointed. She could see Toddy's disapproving face now, not to mention all the Pryce's who had not cared about them until she had started getting medals on the world stage.

Toddy was always bragging about his sister, who was going places. Where was she going now?

Nowhere.

All her efforts to excel in life was all for naught. She was about to be a mother.

She scooped the tests into a bag, tied the bag twice, put it into the trash, and took the trash from the wastebasket. She tied that twice and put it into another bag, which she took out and hid in her closet.

She was acting like a furtive thief in her own apartment, but she didn't want Pete to happen upon her three positive tests.

She was going to pretend like she was fine and that this was an ordinary bout of tiredness. Then tomorrow she would have a quiet word with Amara. Case closed. Baby Pryce Wiley would not exist anymore.

She wouldn't let herself think about it.

She headed downstairs.

Pete was in the kitchen, sitting at the island. He looked so right sitting there like he was meant to be there.

"I started eating." He looked at her intently. "Sorry."

"No problem." Giselle cleared her throat. "Is it good?"

"As usual." Pete nodded, "it's still hot."

Giselle opened her box and got a fork and sat across from him.

He stopped eating. "So?"

"So what?" She asked brightly.

"Are you pregnant?"

"Nope," Giselle said, playing with her rice. She couldn't look at him directly. She concentrated on her food.

Pete sighed. "I don't know if this is bad news or good news. I don't know how to feel."

Giselle inhaled raggedly. "I know. Maybe relief is a good word."

"I don't know, I am not particularly relieved." Pete mused. "I guess it is a good day for you then. You got two scholarships that you have been working for since forever, and best of all you are not pregnant."

Giselle blinked her eyes rapidly.

"Gis, look at me," Pete said, concern rife in his voice.

She couldn't for the life of her raise her head. She didn't even realize that her dratted cheeks were wet until she saw that little droplets of water were working their way into her food.

She felt Pete's arms around her. His chin was in her half-wet hair. "Gis, tell me the truth."

"I am not pregnant." Giselle hiccupped. "I am just tired and stressed out."

Pete hugged her to him. She turned around and threw her arms around his neck. "I am sorry to unload on you like this."

"You can unload on me whenever you feel like it, that's

what I am here for," Pete whispered in her ear. "This was a big scare for us."

Giselle nodded.

"We should just get married." Pete looked at her frankly. "I don't want a scare like this again without you being my wife."

"We are too young." Giselle grabbed a paper towel and wiped her face.

"Says who?" Pete asked urgently. "Gis, we have been living like we are married for close to a year now, you know that if you hadn't gone to Europe this summer, we would have had sex already. My parents know we are having sex."

"You told them!" Giselle widened her eyes. "But why?"

"Because they asked, and I am not into lying to them." Pete frowned, "I don't lie to the people I love."

Giselle turned away feeling like a fraud. She had no problem lying to him.

"So Preston knows, and he hasn't said anything to me?" She whispered. "Wow. I am not coming to your house again."

"Don't be ridiculous." Pete chuckled. "My dad hasn't acted differently toward you, has he?"

"No, but…" Giselle shook her head. She couldn't tell Pete about her pregnancy now. She knew him. She knew that there was no way he would keep his mouth shut about the abortion.

He'd tell Preston. Preston would tell Jordan, those two were thick as thieves. Jordan would tell Sharla. She imagined her whole family ganging up on her and calling her a murderer and a baby killer.

She was feeling guilty just thinking about doing it.

Would she be able to live with herself?

She remembered finding Amara in the locker room at the training center hunched over and crying like her heart was broken after she did it.

That's probably how she would feel.

"Gis?" Pete asked softly. "You sure everything is okay?"

No! Giselle screamed in her head. "I am not hungry," she whispered. Her lips barely able to form the words. "I am going to crash."

She left him sitting in the kitchen. Knowing Pete, he would tidy up. He hated wasting food. The leftovers would go in the fridge. He would load the dishwasher and leave her kitchen sparkling clean. He was incredibly domesticated. A one in a million sort of man. Sensitive, caring, attentive.

He would have made a brilliant father. The thought dogged her all the way upstairs. The Pryce Wiley kid would have been blessed.

****

Pete finished up downstairs. Wiping already clean countertops and thinking. Giselle wasn't acting right. All his senses were on high alert. Her reaction was not normal after she found out she was not pregnant. She would be celebrating. Not crying like her heart was broken.

He looked at the time. It was eight o'clock. Giselle did not go to bed that early. He turned off the kitchen light and headed upstairs. He didn't know why he felt so nervous. Giselle was curled up in the bed in a fetal position. Her hair covered her face like little black cat tails.

Giselle never went to bed with her hair out.

He knew she was crying. He also knew instinctively that she was pregnant. They were pregnant. He was going to be a father. Why would she lie to him though?

He sat on the bed, but she didn't even shift.

"Gis, please don't have an abortion." The word abortion

stuck in his throat. He figured that she was thinking of doing just that.

She curled up in an even tighter ball, which confirmed his fears.

"We can get through this." Pete cleared his throat. "It's not the perfect timing or the best situation, but it's not the worst either. I will take care of the baby while you go and fulfill your dreams."

"It's not your body or your dreams, Pete," Giselle said hoarsely. "You won't be carrying a human being for the next eight months. It won't put a giant full stop in your plans. I didn't plan for any of this."

"I know." Pete sighed, "but I don't think abortion is the answer to this dilemma. You'll only be set back a year."

"A year is a long time. I'll lose my scholarships. I can't train when I am pregnant."

Pete felt himself getting angry. "Giselle, what you can't do is abort my baby because you have your life all planned out, and this child is not in your plans."

Giselle sat up in the bed and stared at him wildly. "It's not your child! That's right. Not yours, and I can do whatever I want with my body. Now get out of my apartment. I don't want to speak to you again. And kindly respect my privacy by not mentioning this to your parents. This has nothing to do with them."

Pete felt like snapping back at her, but he forced himself to calm down. Somebody had to be rational at the moment, and obviously, it was not going to be Giselle.

"Whose child is it?" Pete asked calmly, "who else have you been sleeping with?"

"Kurt!" Giselle growled. "It's his kid. And he'll want me to get rid of it ASAP."

"You never slept with Kurt when you spent a year with him,

hoping to make me jealous, and yet here you are pregnant with his kid." Pete got up. "When did this happen?"

"When did what happen?" Giselle asked, running her fingers through her hair and avoiding his eyes.

"When did you sleep with Kurt? In the summer? When you were both in Europe?" Pete asked each question while still holding himself in check.

"It is none of your business." Giselle inhaled shakily. "We are not in a relationship, remember?"

Pete sighed. It made Giselle feel better to say they were not in a relationship. She knew very well that they were. It gave her some sort of defense to keep repeating it. He let it slide as he let a lot of her little quirks slide. But he wasn't going to let her off the hook with this announcement about her and Kurt.

She needed an excuse to shut him out. He was going to treat this latest announcement as a shut-out tactic. She was trying to get rid of him. He could see her behavior for what it was. He would get angry later, but for now he needed to have his wits about him when he but heads with this headstrong woman.

"If you don't tell me, I'll ask him," Pete said. "I have never thought for one moment that I couldn't trust you. I always thought you were loyal to me. That we were loyal to each other."

Giselle flinched.

"You understand by your behavior and what you are saying that you are choosing your track career and your scholarship over us?" Pete looked at her, dispassionately, "over our child? Over the trust? You are deliberately trying to destroy me, Giselle."

She looked at him, her eyes wide and tear-filled. "Pete, I can't do this…"

Pete felt like strangling her. She was exasperating and maddening, but she was also vulnerable and filled with uncertainty. He doubted that anything he said now would actually be absorbed. He was looking at Giselle in panic mode.

He debated staying with her through the night. She shouldn't be alone.

He exhaled raggedly. He didn't even know he had held in his breath.

"I am staying with you tonight," he said calmly. "You are a wreck."

"I told you it's not your baby," Giselle whispered through bloodless lips.

"I heard you," Pete shrugged, "but you can't know that for sure, can you? I have to be a candidate. We have sex together regularly. Our birth control failed six weeks ago. I am assuming that that is what happened between you and Kurt too?"

Giselle turned her head away. "I guess."

Pete closed his eyes and then opened them. There was a pain that was sitting on his chest. It wasn't subsiding; it was just sitting there.

"You shouldn't put doubt in a man's mind, Gis."

"I know," Giselle murmured, "but this has nothing to do with you. I just want to be left alone."

Pete didn't want to leave. He heard her. He knew he should go and probably howl somewhere. Giselle cheated on him with Kurt, but somehow it didn't ring true. He didn't want to believe it.

"How can you be sure that this baby is Kurt's?" Pete asked some of the exasperation was seeping into his voice. "When did you have the opportunity, the time...I was your first lover, you were mine."

Giselle looked at him sharply. "I made the time."

"You made the time? You made the time!" Pete howled, "Gis! Stop lying because you want to have an abortion! Just stop it, right now!"

Giselle pushed herself further up in the bed a scared look in her face. "Pete, just leave!"

"I will when you tell me the truth," Pete growled.

"I am telling you the truth!" Giselle screamed back at him.

The edges of Pete's vision was turning red. He felt as if he could faint. He was way past angry, and he felt as if Giselle was lying to him.

"Listen to me, Gis. I know this is your body. I know I don't really have a say in what you are going to do, but please know that if this is my child, I want him or her. It will be just a small setback for you if you carry this baby to term."

Giselle sighed and closed her eyes.

"You have options," Pete whispered hoarsely. "Please don't panic and do something stupid. Tell me," Pete blinked back tears, "that you are lying to me about Kurt Yu."

"Could you lock up when you leave?" Giselle asked her voice wan, "I feel so tired."

Pete sighed.

"Just go," Giselle murmured slurring her words as if all the fight had gone out of her.

Pete left. His head was pounding. He felt so distressed he couldn't start the car for a full ten minutes.

****

Pete drove home and sat in the car so long that he was not surprised when his father came out and opened the passenger door.

"What did Giselle do?" Preston asked after looking at his

bloodshot eyes.

"Nothing. Pete inhaled raggedly. "It's what she is about to do that is worrying me. She asked me not to talk about it."

Preston sighed and came into the car. "Okay, you don't have to talk about it. A promise is a promise."

They sat in silence for a while. His father could make him calm without saying a word. That was something that he liked about him.

Pete leaned back his seat even further and closed his eyes. He felt as if someone had dropped him in a meat grinder and forgot to turn off the machine.

"Your grandmother is coming for a visit," Preston said in the silence. "She is staying for a week."

"Cool," Pete said huskily. He liked when Pamela visited. She usually inundated him with stories about when his parents and uncles were younger.

"Your mother had a weird dream the other night." Preston said in the silence, "she dreamt that Giselle had a baby. A boy."

Pete opened his eyes and looked at his father. "Really?"

"She is perturbed by it," Preston said contemplatively. "I said to her that maybe she has babies on the brain. It seems as if all the ladies in here are pregnant. Shawn is due in November, Aisha in December. Lucia is pregnant too. Sandrene recently had Sienna and Sara."

Pete looked at his father's lips as they moved. He had ceased hearing anything since he said Giselle had a baby. A boy?

"Was it mine?" He asked his father. "Did she see this baby's face in the dream?"

Preston shook his head. "She didn't give me that many details. She just said she had the dream. We know you and Giselle are together. We have been antsy ever since."

Pete sighed.

"She is pregnant, isn't she?" Preston asked after a long pause.

"Maybe, she won't be after tomorrow." Pete answered hoarsely, "and maybe the child isn't mine.

"Goodness. Preston murmured. "Oh, my goodness."

"I don't want her to have an abortion Dad,.I don't care if the kid is for someone else, which I highly doubt. I can take care of my child. I can raise my kid. All she has to do is have him."

"You won't need to do it on your own," Preston whispered, "you have us. You'll always have our support."

And then he sighed. "Being a young father is not something I wanted for you. I wanted you to have what me and my brothers never had, two parents, a carefree teenage period, the chance to be responsibility free for a while."

"Maybe, I'll still have all those things," Pete said bitterly. "Giselle is calling the shots."

"Giselle is your kryptonite." Preston sighed, "I should have done something to keep you two apart a long time ago."

Pete squeezed his eyes shut; those pesky tears were threatening to fall again. "I love her. It wouldn't have worked."

"I know," Preston said huskily. "Maybe you are her kryptonite too. I once asked her to leave you alone.

"You did?" Pete looked at his father. "When?"

"When you were sixteen. I could almost predict this happening. Pretty girl, good looking boy, hormones, young love. This had the recipe for trouble written all over it. Why do you think we have so many discussions about sex and protection? I didn't want to be a grandfather while I am still in my thirties. Your mother is going to flip out when she hears this. We were discussing having another child just this morning. But now that being a grandfather is imminent. I think I should talk Giselle out of trying to rob us of having a new life to celebrate."

"You can't get involved or try to intervene," Pete said shakily. "Giselle is crazy enough to go through with this if she senses pressure from anyone. She is in full panic mode. I feel so helpless right now."

"My lips are sealed," Preston said, pain in his voice. "I ache for you."

"I know," Pete said.

"You aren't going to do anything stupid either, are you?" Preston asked fearfully.

"No." Pete laughed humorlessly. "I am just going to call the other paternity candidate and let him know what she is up to."

Chapter Five

Giselle closed her eyes tightly. What had she done?

She wasn't thinking straight, obviously. And she didn't want to think about the here and now and the mess she had just created. She clutched her pillow and tried to think instead of the good times. Ironically, Pete's birthday party came to mind. His sixteenth birthday party.

She had gotten the invitation both physically and by email and had ignored it. Since graduating high school and attending university, she had basically cut off communication with Peter Wiley. He texted her. Sometimes to tell her congratulations when she accomplished something in her track career and as usually, she told him thanks, but that was the extent of it.

She was kind of surprised that he was inviting her to his sixteenth birthday party, and it was going to be in the morning, at ten. It was too early for her. She understood that it was going to be a big deal. The Wiley men were going to make a big production of it.

Her sisters were invited as well, but they weren't going. Tiana was spending her holiday with Sharla and her family in Florida. Elsa had gone to the UK to spend the holidays with the Pryce side of the family.

They had an older sister, Catherine, who was trying to make up for years of ignoring them. A move that coincided with Giselle getting good press because of her athletics. Catherine had invited the three sisters, her especially, but Elsa was the only one who could go.

Toddy had used bribery to get Elsa to go. It may have involved money. Elsa and Toddy were always negotiating some deal or the other.

Giselle had spent the holidays at training camp. She had done it to perfect her hurdling technique, her coaches thought she needed to adjust her strides. It had worked. It had been a grueling fifteen days.

She was just now coming home. Myrna was the only one around. Giselle was thankful for the break and was also looking forward to Myrna's cooking.

She missed her sisters too. In years gone by, they would normally spend the Christmas holidays with her Aunt Sharla and her family at her place in Florida. They were always happy and noisy events.

It was the first holiday the sisters were spending apart. The house was felt empty. She tried to turn on her laptop, but it wouldn't come on. She hadn't used it in the two or so weeks she was away. She was getting exasperated with the thing.

"Argh," she grumbled out loud, slamming the lid shut. "I wanted to check my emails."

"Check it on your phone," Myrna suggested as she flittered around the kitchen fixing breakfast for the two of them.

"I don't check my mail on my phone." Giselle sighed, "I

got nervous about doing it after the incident with Tiana."

"Oh," Myrna grimaced. "The pictures with the teacher. Did they really fire him, what's his name?"

"James Dalton," Giselle answered absently. She was looking at Pete's invitation as if the thing was going to rise up and bite her.

Myrna caught her looking at it and decided to go into her preachy mode. "I can't believe you. This whole track thing has taken over your life. You are too dedicated. Why do you even do it anyway? It's not like you need to, you have a rich brother who will give you anything. You work too hard."

Giselle grunted. "Oh, Myrna. Toddy will not be around forever. I can't be a leech. I have to be independent."

"Don't oh, Myrna me," Myrna snorted. "You are too young to be missing out on so much in life. You train day and night for what, a little trophy? When it's all said and done, when your youth has passed, then what?"

Giselle made a face. "You are giving me the exact opposite of a pep talk."

"I think you should go and live it up like your sisters." Myrna looked at her, concerned.

"Has anybody ever told you that you resemble the mother in that show, Family Matters? What's her name again?"

"Harriette Winslow." Myrna smiled, "you are not going to change the subject on me, Giselle. I am worried about you."

"I am fine." Giselle sighed, "I finished training camp without an injury. Happy new year to me."

"Go to the party." Myrna insisted. "Spend time with that side of your family. Have some fun. Please."

Giselle sighed. "I don't know why he invited me to his party. It's not as if we are still friends. I could do with a long peaceful nap. My new year's resolution is to sleep more."

Myrna glared at her. "You are just eighteen years old."

"I will be nineteen in nine days." Giselle corrected, "This is the only time of the year when Pete is a mere two years younger than I am."

"Get out of the house. Do something fun. I don't even care if it's at the party," Myrna said, your life is no sort of life at all."

"What did you do for the holiday?" Giselle asked.

Myrna put a plate of the omelet in front of her with all the trimmings and then sat across from her.

"I went to visit my parents in the country. My sisters and brothers, nieces and nephews and all the family were there. We are large and close-knit. It was fun."

"Your parents are still alive?" Giselle tucked into the omelet and closed her eyes in ecstasy. "Nobody does an omelet like you."

"Thanks." Myrna smiled. "And yes, my parents are still alive. They have a long ways to go too. They are not in their dotage. My mom had me when she was pretty young. I am the second of ten."

"Wow." Giselle widened her eyes.

"Yup." Myrna laughed, "She had me at seventeen, my dad was seventeen too. They married when they were sixteen."

"Are you serious? Giselle gasped, "and they are still together?"

"Oh, yes." Myrna nodded, "and they are loyal to each other."

"That's rare." Giselle whistled. "Like I can't even imagine that."

"They had the real thing." Myrna mused. "They knew each other as children. They were neighbors. They grew up together and then got married in my grandparent's backyard. That's the way they did it in those days."

"Why didn't you ever marry?" Giselle asked. She finished

the omelet and licked her lips.

"I have the gift of singleness." Myrna smiled. "I am fine the way I am. I will go back to the earth the same way I was born, untouched by a man."

"What if Mr. Right comes along?" Giselle teased. "What are you going to do then?"

"He has to be very right." Myrna mused. "And he can't interfere with my ministry. I think I was called to work with people who are on their way out of this life, sick people, people who are dying. I bring them cheer and comfort. I tell them of Jesus' love and read and sing to them."

Giselle widened her eyes. "I didn't know that."

"You are oblivious to everything else but your training and your schoolwork." Myrna tucked her hand under her chin. "Did you know that Tiana still feels sorry about getting that poor teacher fired."

Giselle nodded. "Yes, I know that is all she talks about. Technically she didn't get him fired, they decided to fire him after the pictures that they found on her stolen phone."

"Okay, I'll give you that one," Myrna scrunched up her face in consternation. "Did you know that Elsa acts the way she does because she is seeking attention, namely Toddy's. He is the reason why she is so outlandish; her heart is not into most of the shenanigans she gets up to. She is more into acceptance from family than either you or Tiana."

"No, she's not." Giselle chuckled. "Elsa is a law onto herself. She dances to her own beat.

"She is crying out for attention," Myrna murmured," just like you with this track thing and your over-achieving ways. It's just that all of you manifest it differently. I told Toddy that you three need therapy."

"I have no time for therapy." Giselle grimaced. "The therapist is going to say that I have a Type A personality and that I need to relax. I will relax when I am dead."

"Type A?" Myrna raised her eyebrows, "what's that?"

Giselle opened her mouth.

"Wait, don't tell me," Myrna got up and reached for her phone. "I can ask my smartphone."

Giselle rolled her eyes. Since Myrna discovered that she could ask her smartphone anything, she was like a kid with a toy.

"Type A personality," Myrna said to the phone and waited with glee, while it spoke.

The computer voice came on: Type A personality, a temperament characterized by excessive ambition, aggression, competitiveness, drive, impatience, need for control. It is commonly associated with risk of coronary disease and other stress-related ailments.

"Oh goodness," Myrna made a sign of the cross and kissed her fingers. "You need help. I have a cousin, Barry Perkins, he is a therapist. You must have heard me mention him before. I am going to invite him over for lunch since you will be here."

Giselle jumped up. "I won't be here. I am going to Pete's party."

Myrna looked at her aghast. "But Giselle, your personality sounds as if it will kill you. All of the things the computer listed is true. It's you."

"Not all of it, I am not aggressive."

"Yes, you are." Myrna nodded. "You are like a dog with a bone when you have an idea. You never give things a rest. This explains why you are always so regimented, and everything has to be perfect. Everything has to be just right, or you go crazy. You have never gotten anything less than an A, and if you come second in a race, you come home crying that you lost."

"Number two is not number one," Giselle grunted.

"You need help." Myrna clapped her head. "If anyone can help you, my cousin Barry can."

Giselle shook her head. "I think I am halfway cured. See, I am going to the party."

Myrna shrugged. "We'll see. It's the right step. Wear a dress. And remember your bathing suit. It says so on the invitation."

Giselle groaned. "Okay."

"Hurry up." Myrna glanced at the clock. "You'll be late."

****

Myrna tricked her into coming to Pete's party. Giselle thought when she drove into the Wiley complex. Myrna knew that the very word psychiatrist would trigger her to leave the house.

She wound down her window and parked behind Guy's car. The place was jammed with cars. It was a huge party.

She exited her vehicle reluctantly and almost ran into Aisha, Walter's wife. She was dressed in a white summer dress and had a straw hat perched on her head.

"Hey Giselle," Aisha greeted her warmly.

"Hey," Giselle cleared her throat. "It's pretty busy around here."

Aisha nodded. "The bus is around the parking lot."

"Bus?" Giselle tried not to let her surprise be shown. "But what bus?"

She grabbed her tote bag from the car and rummaged through it for the invitation. It said, come and join Pete at the waterpark in St. Ann. From eleven to four. Food and drinks all day. RSVP Please.

Why hadn't she seen all of that? Why had she thought

poolside and the Wiley Complex, with maybe her cousins and some of Pete's friends from school?

She shouldn't have come.

What was Georgia doing today? She could go and hang with her and when a suitable time had passed, then go back home. Maybe she could get some advanced studying done, she had Physics next semester. The dreaded Physics. She had gotten a B for it in her overall grade at high school, and it had made her angry for days.

Another symptom of her Type A personality coming back to haunt her. She only got A's. She would rather prepare for the Physics class than go to Pete's party in St. Ann. She wished she had read the thing. She was usually spot on with her attention to detail.

She headed back to the car. She was always welcomed at Georgia's place.

"Gis!" It was Pete's voice.

She spun around guiltily. "Oh, hey Pete. Happy Birthday!"

She hoped she was saying it as casually as she could because she was feeling slightly breathless. Pete was no longer the Pete that she was used to seeing. She hadn't seen him for close to a year, and he had grown taller. His shoulders were broader, and he had muscles. He had honest to goodness muscles that he was showing off in his sleeveless gray shirt and blue jeans shorts.

His face had lost all the roundedness, and he now had more angles and planes. Had his lips always been that deep pink?

He was quite stunning. Giselle leaned on the car to gain her balance. Peter Wiley had thrown her off balance.

He grinned at her. "Thank you for coming, you never RSVPed, and I was kinda disappointed about that. I debated calling you and personally begging you to come, but I have some pride left."

Giselle roused herself out of her stupor to ask, "What does that mean…some pride left."

"You blanked me." Pete pushed his hand in his pocket. "Froze me out."

"Oh," Giselle cleared her throat. "Yeah."

"But you are here now," Pete said. "You can sit beside me on the bus. Come on, we leave in five minutes."

Giselle grasped her bag closer to her and shook her head. "I had no idea that we were going to St. Ann, of all places. I never really looked at the invitation. I thought it was a pool party."

Pete wrinkled his brow. "You are not going to chicken out on this, Gis. If you don't come, I won't go either. Think of my parents and my uncles. They planned this for me. They rented a entire waterpark just for my friends and me to have fun. You'll ruin this for everybody."

Giselle glared at him. "I wouldn't want to ruin everybody's fun."

He held out his hands for hers, and she took it reluctantly.

When he laced their fingers together and pulled her even closer to him. She knew she was in trouble.

Pete looked down at her and smiled. "Now, my birthday will be happy."

****

The day would stand out for Giselle because of two things. She actually had fun. She couldn't remember being genuinely relaxed in her life. Usually, her mind was ticking over a mile a minute, but she had no time to think. She went on all the slides. Actually hung out with Pete's friends, a mixed crowd of boys and girls and ate junk food. She would pay for it in training, but somehow, she didn't care.

All her cousins were there. She got a chance to have long conversations with each of them. Jordan had her in stitches when he told her stories about her mother.

"I loved aunt Monique." Jordan looked at her fondly. "She was like my mom's second mom. You know you guys lived in the perfect paradise. Man, we used to love going to her place. I wonder what Toddy did with it? Last time I enquired, he had plans to sell it to a developer."

"Tell me more about our grandmother." Giselle shivered, she was in a red bikini, but she shrugged on a wrap, the day was bordering on chilly. She only felt it when she sat down, though. The water was warm and inviting.

"Our grandmother, Iris Kennedy." Jordan made a face. "She left her three girls with her husband and never looked back. She just got up one day and disappeared. And then our grandfather died mysteriously and Monique, being the oldest girl took over."

"I wonder what happened to our grandmother," Giselle mused. "Have you ever tried to find her?"

"No." Jordan shook his head. "I never even thought about it. To be honest, I haven't thought much about that side of our family. If you want to know more speak to Sharla. She mentioned once that she was searching for her mother."

"Okay." Giselle made a face, "Aunt Sharla thinks I don't keep in touch enough. She needs to live my life to understand."

"You are so focused it is almost scary," Jordan looked at her proudly. "I am proud of you. I don't know where you get that work ethic and that drive from. You could be taking things easy."

"Thanks." Giselle smiled. "Taking it easy is not in my DNA."

"Our mothers would be pleased." Jordan nodded. "You

know you look a lot like my mom?"

"I heard." Giselle made a face. "And Pete looks a lot like your Dad."

"Well, he does. He looks like Preston and me." Jordan nodded. "My goodness, I never thought of it before, but you two could be young Hannah Kennedy and Joseph Wiley."

Giselle thought better of pursuing that thought in a conversation. Hannah Kennedy and Joseph Wiley had been young lovers who had not let Joseph's marriage or children with his wife get in the way of them being together. She didn't want Jordan associating her and Pete with being in a relationship.

She changed the subject instead.

"I wonder how our grandmother looked. I wonder what would make a woman just up and leave her children. She shouldn't have had them in the first place."

"If she hadn't," Jordan said, "we wouldn't be here. I like being here."

He waved to Shawn who was in the shallow part of the water with their baby girl, Courtney.

"I can't believe that you two are still in love after all this time." Giselle shook her head.

"I'll never get enough of her," Jordan said dreamily, "I'll love her till the day I die."

Giselle blinked away tears, he said it with such simple passion. It made her teary and envious at the same time.

After her conversation with Jordan, she was swept up in a beach volleyball competition with Pete as her partner against his parents, Preston and Sheryl. She and Pete won. But just barely.

"I didn't think we would win against an international track star." Sheryl laughed after the game was done. "And Pete is freakishly limber. But we did good, didn't we babe?"

Preston nodded. He dropped a hand around his wife's waist. "Yes, we did. That, and we had to let them win, it's Pete's birthday."

Pete grinned. "Yeah, right."

Preston and Sheryl went for drinks at one of the bars, and Pete looked at her. "Enjoying yourself?"

"Surprisingly, yes." Giselle nodded. "It's always nice to be around family."

"We should be friends again," Pete said casually. "I won't have an obvious crush on you again. Therefore you won't need to let me down harshly and break my heart.

"You had a crush on me?" Giselle smiled. "Really, now?"

"Oh, yes." Pete inhaled raggedly. "I ate, slept and dreamed Giselle Pryce. I was a wreck. You know I learned violin for you. I haven't picked it up since. Remember that day when you told me that you were interested in your trainer, Kurt and that I was too young to be having thoughts about you."

"I never said that," Giselle protested.

"It was something like that," Pete spun the ball on his pointing finger, "I went home, and I cried. No, forget that. I didn't wait until I got home to cry. I cried on my way home. I cried all that week. My mom and dad took me to the doctor."

Giselle widened her eyes. "Are you serious?"

"Dead serious." Pete chuckled. "I went to the doctor because of you. I had it bad. I avoided you at school too, but of course, you didn't notice. Are you and Kurt still together?"

"We weren't together." Giselle's head was still reeling from Pete's confession. She had noticed that he was avoiding her after that evening when she had let him down and had felt like crying too.

"I have a girlfriend now." Pete shrugged, "do you know Esther Bollings?"

"Yep." Giselle nodded. "A pinprick of jealousy had her in

its clutches. She is in some of my classes at university. Her father is a pastor."

"At my church," Pete said dreamily, "we sing on the choir together."

"She is older than you," Giselle growled.

"It seems as if I have a thing for older women." Pete chuckled at her expression. "We do duets, you should come hear us."

Giselle looked down at the sand. She had the insane urge to cry. "What was the matter with her?" She blinked away the tears.

"I might come." She said her voice choked up. "I haven't gone to church in a while."

She didn't hear when Pete moved closer to her. She felt when he touched her hair.

"Gis, we can be friends again, can't we?"

"Sure, why not?" She looked up at him brightly, and then a diabolical part of her wanted to get back at him. "I'll bring one of my boyfriends along."

"Boyfriends? As in more than one?" Pete looked perplexed. "I had no idea you had so much time on your hands. I came and watched you at training the other day. You work hard."

"There are a lot of things you don't know about me," Giselle said disparagingly.

"Apparently." Pete looked at her, intently. "Anyway, don't sell yourself short. You are too precious for that."

Giselle looked at him in confusion. "What do you mean?"

"I mean, you are gorgeous and sweet and funny. Don't have too many boyfriends. You need just one. One who will love and appreciate you because of who you are. I miss you sometimes. I used to love our chats at night."

Giselle cleared her throat.

"I was lying about the boyfriends. I was kind of jealous

about Esther."

"You were?" Pete grinned. "Good, because I was lying about Esther. We broke up. If we were together, she would be here. I deliberately didn't invite her because I invited you. I wanted you to come. I needed you to come."

Giselle frowned. "I never thought of that. I went into instant jealous mode, which I shouldn't because…"

"We are just friends and mean absolutely nothing to each other," Pete said.

"Something like that." Giselle cleared her throat. "So what do you do in your free time these days?"

"Computer apps, games mostly." Pete chuckled. "I seem to have a natural knack for it. I have a game out, it's doing well. It shocked my dad how well it was doing. I am making money in my room. Lots of it. He said it is baffling him."

"Well, congrats." Giselle giggled. "I can see Preston being perplexed about it. I imagine he wanted you in the supermarket business."

Pete nodded. "I might still do that, but I much prefer working with computers. I am the one who my uncles and the aunts bring their gadget issues to. I worked on an app for uncle Jordan. It's so useful to him, he actually paid me for it. And uncle Walter helped me to set up my own business, it's called Wiley Apps."

"Wiley Apps," Giselle said it slowly. "It sounds good. I am having issues with my laptop, it won't start. Can you help me with that?"

"Sure. Pete shrugged, "bring it over, I'll run a diagnostic on it. I'll be going back to school in two weeks. I have the time."

"Okay." Giselle nodded. "Will tomorrow be okay?"

Pete nodded. "I'll tell my parents you'll be stopping by. I am going to have to convince my mother that you won't break my heart again."

"Pete…"

Pete grinned. "Don't worry, I'll convince her that I am good. I will never assume or overstep my boundaries with you again. I swear."

"I…I…" Giselle looked into his limpid brown eyes and realized that she couldn't promise the same. She liked him! It was frightening how much.

"Over here, Pete," Walter called. He had assembled a group for a picture.

"And Giselle!" Walter waved them over.

"Let's go, we have a picture to take." Pete grabbed her hand, and she briefly squeezed them.

She didn't miss the look that he sent her when she did that or the fact that he hastily pulled his hand away.

Chapter Six

The next day, promptly at eight she was out the door with her computer in hand. Toddy was hung over from an all-night new year's eve party and was slowly sipping tomato juice in the kitchen.

He waved at her in a sad, forlorn gesture. His son, Lincoln, was laughing and talking with Myrna.

And she heard a crash in the pantry which meant that Kaylon, Lincoln's horror child was around.

Lincoln was Toddy's eldest son. He was a lawyer and Toddy's golfing buddy. He lived nearby, and he was obviously dressed and ready for the course and waiting patiently for Toddy to get over his new year's celebration. Knowing Toddy, he may have gone to more than one party, trying to please everyone on his social calendar.

"Giselle," Lincoln spotted her first. "I haven't seen you since last year."

Giselle grinned. Lincoln made the same joke every year.

It felt odd to think of Lincoln as her nephew. He was in his late forties. He had a ten-year-old son, Kaylon who called her Grand Aunty Gis.

Giselle was glad to escape the house, if Kaylon was over it was going to be chaos for the day. He did not know the meaning of the word no.

The little boy was a terror who had the attention span of a gnat. Kaylon made her happy she did not have younger siblings.

"Where are you going, Aunty Gis?" Lincoln asked, laughing. He called her aunty in fun. It was his greatest delight to introduce her and Tiana and Elsa as his aunts. He loved to watch as people acted confused because he was way older than them.

"To the Wiley's." Giselle said, "Pete is going to help me with something."

"Ah," Lincoln nodded, "the Wiley's. I did some business with Jordan the other day. Tell him hello from me, if you see him."

"How was the party yesterday?" Myrna asked, "you came in so late."

"She came in late from a party?" Toddy whispered. "Whose party?"

"Peter Wiley," Myrna said softly.

"Oh," Toddy massaged his temples. "I should give him a present. Lincoln give him a present."

Lincoln looked perplexed. "What kind of present?"

"Your wallet." Toddy placed his empty glass of tomato juice on his forehead and rolled it around. "How old is the kid?"

"Sixteen," Giselle said.

"Sixteen?" Toddy turned bloodshot eyes to Giselle. "I got Lincoln's mother pregnant when I was sixteen. Who will be at the house today except you and this kid?"

"The housekeeper," Giselle said, "and nobody is getting me pregnant."

Toddy grunted. "I feel like hell warmed over, or I would argue with you. I know how sixteen-year-old boys think. I was sixteen once. Lincoln was sixteen once. Take Kaylon with you."

"Are you kidding me?" Giselle screeched. "You want to get rid of Kaylon. You are not saddling me with him."

An accompanying crash in the pantry had Toddy wincing. "It was worth a try. Myrna says she is going to quit if I leave him here with her."

"That's right," Myrna said. "I think that boy needs therapy. He has attention deficit disorder."

Giselle snorted. "Myrna thinks everybody needs therapy."

"But she is right, though." Lincoln shrugged, "Unfortunately my wife says, Kaylon is perfect the way he is, I just need to spend more quality time with him."

Giselle giggled. "Bye, guys. Spend quality time with your offspring."

"Wait!" Toddy winced because he had to raise his voice. "I need to give Pete a present."

Another crash in the pantry, this time accompanied by a loud squeal, had Toddy holding his head.

"Lincoln, go check on that boy. Myrna if he has broken his legs will you take him for the day? He'd be in one place. Immobile. He can't get in trouble when he can't walk."

"I don't know," Myrna looked thoughtful. "His hands would be free. How much extra are you paying me?"

Kaylon ran into the kitchen. He was covered in wine. "I found the Christmas fruit! I think I broke a bottle...they won't open!"

"You didn't have any, did you?" Myrna looked shocked.

Preston and continued with her breakfast prepping.

"It won't start."

Sheryl turned around. "Please don't hurt my baby. There is nothing like first love, and you are his first love. As his mother, I wish he didn't have to go through this, but I understand that this is a part of growing up. You have that boy's heart in your hands. Please, Giselle, handle it with care."

Giselle nodded uncertainly. "I will."

Pete came downstairs with a bundle of cords in his hand. "Gis! Where is that laptop? Let's get started."

She looked at him, dressed casually in black, a smile across his pink lips and wondered wildly, who was going to caution Pete not to hurt her?

****

She and Pete had been practically joined at the hip since he fixed her laptop. She had been a regular fixture over at his house, always under the watchful eye of one or both of his parents who hadn't quite relaxed around her. It was baffling because Pete didn't act like a person who would fall apart if she blanked him again.

She was the one who was feeling anxious about him. He had grown to mean a lot to her. They kept in touch for most of the day and generally acted like two people in a relationship.

She had participated in all fourteen Diamond League events that year and had made the finals for all her events. She had even made it to first place more than once and had accumulated quite a bit of prize money.

Her coach, Stevens, was happy with her and then he got an overseas offer at a university in Florida, and he asked her to come with him.

She had initially thought to refuse. It was a no brainer. She wasn't ready to leave Jamaica, but she told Toddy and her sisters about it first.

They were at the kitchen table, where they usually held their family meetings.

Tiana scrunched up her face in consternation. "You should go. I was thinking about moving to Florida myself. Aunt Sharla would be ecstatic."

"No," Toddy drummed his fingers on the table, "you should all stay here and come work in the company with me. I am having some difficulty keeping business around with Mason Magnus yapping at my feet. That boy is out to ruin me. Maybe I'll have to downsize a bit or merge."

"It can't be that bad." Elsa frowned. "Mousy Mason is not out to ruin you."

"I don't know what gave you the idea that Mason Magnus is mousy. He is a shark. A bloodthirsty shark who has me up for sins I supposedly committed against his mother. He is siphoning off business from me, and I hear he is plotting for my Senate seat."

"He is just twenty-six," Elsa shrugged off Toddy's alarm. "You can nip his enthusiasm in the bud."

"I don't know," Toddy said fretfully. "He is talking to all the right people. Whispering in their ears, getting the big contracts, and expanding at a rapid pace. I underestimated him for a while, thinking he was just full of youthful exuberance and had no bite, but now, I am sadly mistaken. I feel vulnerable."

Giselle looked at Toddy sharply. He didn't admit weaknesses aloud unless he was apprehensive.

He seemed to realize what he had done and tried to put some levity back in his speech. "I should be retiring soon anyway. The advertising world is becoming too fast paced for me. Some days I find myself daydreaming about Caymanas

Golf Club. I have a house near there. I could sell this one. You three will be gone soon anyway…I could downscale my life."

"I hate when you get broody." Elsa scowled.

"And morbid." Tiana frowned. "If you sell the house, where would we go?"

Toddy chuckled. "I won't sell the house or the business yet. I will hold on to them until I breathe my last breath, or until poverty knocks on my door."

"I wouldn't mind working in advertising when I am finished with school," Elsa mused. "We could fight Mason Magnus together."

"At least one girl is thinking straight." Toddy grinned.

Giselle cleared her throat. "We started out talking about me, Giselle Pryce. My coach is leaving for Florida, and he asked me to go with him. All those in favor of me going show hands."

Only Tiana raised her hand.

Giselle made a face. "Okay, then, I'll stay."

"What does Pete say?" Elsa asked cheekily. "Surely your other half should have a say in this."

Toddy looked at her sharply. "I didn't know you two were dating."

"We are not." Giselle drummed her fingers on the table. "We are just friends."

And then she changed the subject quickly. "I am going to have to ask Kurt Yu to coach me if Stevens leaves."

"I like him," Elsa said. "He is cute."

"And professional." Giselle responded, "that's why I have worked with him these last couple years. Who cares if he is cute?"

Toddy nodded. "Now that's the right attitude. I am happy that you are staying. I will retire when you three are happily married and off the market. Then I'll consider my work done."

Elsa laughed. "I am never getting married."

Tiana giggled. "You are crazy."

Giselle imagined herself in a white dress in a wedding chapel somewhere with Pete as her groom.

She closed her eyes to rid herself of the image.

Elsa threw her a speculative look but said nothing.

Giselle groaned inwardly, Elsa observant Elsa was going to take note of her response and be on her case later.

****

Giselle found her way to Pete's house that night. She didn't even bother with an excuse anymore. She just showed up whenever she was in the area, which was anytime she felt like hanging with Pete. This was her unwind station. Sometimes she watched television with the family. Sometimes she hung with Pete at the poolside.

Preston had humorlessly said that they should give her a key. The security never bothered to ask her any questions anymore. He just let her into the complex.

She texted Pete when she drove in and was greeted by him at the door. He was dressed up in black pants and a long-sleeved white shirt. He looked cool and fresh and better every time she saw him. He grinned at her when she exited the car.

"I have choir practice tonight. You can take me. I'll tell my mom that she doesn't have to bother."

"It wasn't a bother." Sheryl peered through the door. "But since Giselle is here, go with her. I can't wait until you are old enough to drive yourself."

"Hey Gis," Sheryl greeted her warmly. The hostility and

guardedness had long dissipated. Sheryl treated her like a sister or a close friend.

"Come on," Giselle inclined her head to Pete, "let's go then."

Pete kissed his mother on the cheek. "Have fun. I'll be fine. I live in an entire complex filled with uncles and aunties. I won't burn the house down or throw parties. Miss Blossom will be here on Monday. The house will be standing when you get back."

"Thanks, my love." Sheryl waved them goodbye and hurried away.

"What's going on?" Giselle asked when they were in the car. "What's the hurry with Sheryl?"

"It's my parent's anniversary, and they are spending the week in Belize." Pete chuckled. "Dad told mom to pack light because they were not going to be needing much clothes."

Giselle giggled. "Really?"

"Yup." Pete nodded, "so they are leaving Petra with Aunt Aisha and Uncle Walter. I'll have the house to myself."

"Is that so?" Giselle raised an eyebrow. "I hope you are not inviting any girls over."

"Nope." Pete shook his head. "There is only one girl for me. No, pluralization."

Giselle glanced at him. He didn't even look at her while he was saying it.

"Pete…"

"Yes, Giselle." He finally turned to her.

"You are not catching feelings for me or anything like that, are you?"

"No," Pete said gravely, "I am not."

"Good." Giselle sighed; she drove out of the complex and turned in the direction of the church.

"I can't catch feelings for you," Pete said in the silence.

"I've always had them. I'll probably always will. I've had them since I met you. It was like being knocked sideways. My feelings for you are a very present and real part of me."

Giselle slowed to a crawl. "You are too young to know that."

"I told my dad that I loved you when I was thirteen and he went silent, and then he said he understood. He didn't tell me I couldn't or that I am too young. He said that's the same way he felt about my mom when he was my age. It laid dormant when they were apart for a while, but it never went away. When he saw her again, it flared up again. I don't think this will die, Gis."

Giselle cleared her throat. "I thought we were just friends."

"You have never thought so," Pete said confidently. "You are attracted to me. I can see it. I can feel it. I knew it from the very first time we saw each other."

"Let's talk about something else," Giselle said hurriedly.

"I promised my dad I wouldn't act on my feelings for you until I am eighteen. He begged me to wait. You are safe for now. You have one year and three months left." Pete smiled at her. "I am serious about my promises. My dad knows he can take me at my word."

"You are sure of yourself!" Giselle sputtered. "What on earth gave you the idea that I will just sit around and wait for you to act on it."

She turned into the church parking lot and turned to Pete, her eyes fierce. "I am going to be seeing other people. This thing between us is getting out of hand."

"Okay." Pete shrugged. "See other people or whatever. I'll see other people too."

Giselle's lips trembled. "Pete, this is crazy."

Pete touched her face lightly. It was just a light touch; she felt it all the way down to the apex of her thighs. She clamped her leg shut.

Pete watched her and then sighed. "Practice is an hour, you staying? If not, I am going to have to call one of my uncles to pick me up."

Giselle made a face. "Maybe, I should go home."

"Or maybe you should stay," Pete said. "We could hang out after this, listen to your favorite songs..."

"My coach is leaving Jamaica, wants me to come with him," Giselle said in a rush. "It wouldn't be a hard transition. I have the grades and the university loves my resume."

Pete came back to the car and sat down. He turned to her fully. "You would leave me?"

"I am thinking about my career and my studies," Giselle said, "this decision has nothing to do with you."

Pete picked up the plait of hair that she had over her shoulders and pulled her closer to him.

"Pete..." Giselle looked at him as if he had lost his senses, but all she saw were his spiky eyelashes over limpid brown eyes.

Pete was as still as possible, he looked as if he was drinking her in. "Gis, I don't want a long-distance relationship."

He wrapped her hair over and over in his hands and gently tugged her close to his lips, and then he kissed her.

They kissed until they were breathing hard. The car glass was fogged up.

"Where'd you learn to kiss like that?" Giselle asked her lips were throbbing and swollen.

"I have been practicing with you in my imagination." Pete laughed, dryly. "I just never imagined that it would be in the church parking lot."

"We can't repeat this." Giselle's voice was husky. She looked at his lips. She wanted to feel it on hers again. "And we are not in a relationship."

"Aren't we?" Pete smiled, lifting only one side of his lips in mockery. "I don't know, Giselle. What we have certainly feels like it."

Chapter Seven

Present Day

"**Y**ou okay this morning?" Kurt asked Giselle as soon as she stepped into the training center. He was sitting at the receptionist desk because she hadn't come into work yet. It was still early.

"Right as rain," Giselle said chirpily. She didn't want to tell him that she had puked her guts out this morning or that she was only in because Amara was not answering her phone. Tiana had dropped off her car in the morning, and she had tried to avoid her sister by hiding in the bathroom until she left. She hadn't slept much last night. Guilt and uncertainty were eating her up.

She had tried to hide her tear-swollen eyes this morning by applying a cold compress and using eye drops and putting cucumbers on her eyes, but she still looked a little puffy around the eyes. Definitely, a dead giveaway that everything was not all right. She tried to evade Kurt's speculative gaze, but he was determined to drag out their conversation.

"So what are you doing here this morning? I thought you weren't on the roster until evening."

"I am here to see Amara." Giselle gritted out. "She is on morning rotation, isn't she?"

Kurt had a way of looking at her with a laser-sharp gaze as if he could see all her secrets. "She is in the locker room," Kurt said. His phone rang at the same time, and it gave her a chance to escape him.

Amara was in the locker room alone. Changing into her workout gear.

"Hey you," She grinned at Giselle, "I have not seen you for a minute. What's up?"

"I need the name of your doctor," Giselle said, looking around to make sure that they were alone.

"Which one?" Amara asked, pulling her shirt over her head and ruffling her hair. She ran her fingers through her curls uncaringly and then turned to Giselle.

"The one," Giselle said solemnly. "I am six weeks along."

"Don't do it." Amara shook her head, "It's not worth it. My husband left me because of it. I had to go to counseling. I still think about it. It's a mental drain."

"I don't want advice," Giselle sighed, "I just want to get this over and done with."

"I know that sense of urgency, that get it over and done with feeling," Amara looked at her with sympathy in her eyes. "But at the end of the day, it is not worth it. The regret is real."

"The name Amara," Giselle said firmly.

"Baxter," Amara said glumly. "He is in the phone book. You have to tell him that you were raped. It makes him feel better about it. There is another one Felix, he doesn't ask questions. Everything is off the books, but he is expensive."

"Thanks." Giselle nodded.

"You know this is messed up, right." Amara asked fiercely, "choosing a career in tracks above your own flesh and blood."

"I know." Giselle sighed, "but I have spent so much time at this thing. I gave up holidays and fun things, I gave up a good chunk of my life…"

"What does all of this matter?" Amara whispered, "a trophy, some money, notoriety? I ask myself this every day. At the end of the day, you are going to ask yourself the same thing. You may not like the answer. And this will haunt you, mark my words."

"It matters," Giselle said stubbornly.

She left the locker room and almost bumped into Kurt.

He glared at her. "You are pregnant?"

"How'd you know that?" Giselle gasped.

"Just heard from Pete," Kurt growled. "He wanted to know if you told me that you were aborting my child. I was so surprised that I don't remember what I told him."

Giselle shook her head. "I am not talking about this."

"To my office, now." Kurt pointed to his door down the corridor. "I am your coach, this is important. You signed a contract that said you have to tell me these things."

He stormed down the corridor to his office and held the door open. Giselle followed him reluctantly.

Kurt closed the door and glared at her. "I don't know where I should start. The last time I checked you proudly declared that you weren't having sex without marriage. You put a ban on heavy petting between us when we were together, and now, I am your baby's father? A whole year after we broke up?"

"I had to tell Pete something. He was determined that I should keep this baby, and I don't want to."

"I knew that boy was trouble." Kurt shook his head. "He

seduced you, didn't he?"

"No." Giselle plonked down in one of the chairs around Kurt's desk. "And no, I don't want to discuss this."

"But alas, you'll have to." Kurt sat across from her. "I am involved. Why use me as your scapegoat?"

"Because you would support me to do whatever I want to do to push my career forward. Besides, who else was I supposed to tell Pete was my child's father?"

Kurt stared at her unblinkingly for several seconds.

"Say something." Giselle urged. "Tell me I am doing the right thing for my career."

Kurt folded his arms. "I want to tell you just that, but I heard Pete over the phone, and he is broken. I know what it feels like when you break someone."

"I don't break people," Giselle said, feeling two inches tall.

"Oh, Gis, you do. Nobody and nothing comes between your determination to be superwoman. You are formidable. You have a one-track mind that is actually frightening. Once you have made up your mind about something, you scare me."

"I am not that bad," Giselle whispered hoarsely.

"Take me, for instance," Kurt leaned forward, "you used me to make the boy jealous, and I went along with you. Little did I know that when Giselle Pryce decides she is in love with someone else, you don't stand a chance. You strung me along until Pete forced you to choose between us."

Giselle swallowed. "That's not quite how it went."

"Oh, it wasn't," Kurt raised his eyebrows.

"No," Giselle said impatiently, "anyway, can we get back to the point at hand?"

"Oh," Kurt mused, "you want me to lie to the boy that you and I are having a torrid affair and that you are carrying my child and I have no qualms about you getting rid of my child

I knew his life deserved a chance, But everybody told me to be smart, Look at your career they said, Lauryn, baby use your head, But instead I chose to use my heart

It was a song about not aborting her son Zion. Giselle turned off the radio, but the song kept repeating in her head. Now the joy of my world is Zion.

Giselle was happy when she saw the house through the windscreen. It looked foggy in the distance, and she realized that it was because she had tears in her eyes.

She parked and heaved a sigh of relief. She was not turning on the radio again today. It seemed as if God was trying to get her attention by whatever means necessary. She wasn't going to feel guilty. She was going through with the abortion. She would confess her sins later and clean up her life. She had already lost Pete, so no more premarital sex for her. After this, she would dot all the I's and cross all the t's. She would even go back to church.

Her next foray into motherhood would happen when she was thirty or so after she had met a man who had all of Pete's qualities and who she loved like she loved Pete. She would get married first. This was after she got her med degree and was practicing and had a couple of world and Olympic medals under her belt.

That was the plan. Surely God would understand and forgive her this. She didn't mean for any of this to happen. But was that true, though? Was this really an accident?

Chapter Eight

A year and a half ago…

Pete was becoming too attached to her. And her to him. He even came to watch her train in the mornings, and he was madly jealous of Kurt.

"Does he have to be your coach?" Pete asked after watching her train in February.

"Yes." Giselle stretched near him and panted. "What's wrong with him?"

"He looks at you too…" Pete shrugged, "I don't know… familiar."

Giselle giggled. She liked it when Pete was jealous and showed it. Usually, she was the one who was insanely jealous of him. The church choir members treated him like a rock star, and all the girls fawned over him.

There was one girl in particular that made Giselle grit her teeth every time she visited Pete's church; her name was Rylee. She sang beautifully, she had a lot in common with

Pete, they went to the same high school and were in the same classes and worked on computer apps together.

He was an anomaly among his peers. He was polite, respectful and he had an odd way of making a person the center of his attention as if they were the only person in the world to him.

"Where'd you get it from?" Giselle sat beside him and asked.

"What?" Pete asked, smiling.

"The focus thing. I can never complain that you are not paying attention. You are always here in the moment."

"That's a good thing, right?" Pete raised an eyebrow.

"It is." Giselle smiled. "It is kind of old school. You are not on your phone or texting someone. You have an old soul."

"Or," Pete licked his pink lips, "I was raised by people who emphasized that it is polite to listen when you are with someone and give them your attention. My dad and uncles are good role models. I spend a lot of time with them when I am not with you."

Kurt chose that moment to come over, and he stood looking between the two of them. "Peter Wiley. You are here every day. Why don't you join the track team?"

Pete stood up. "I am not interested."

"I hope you are not distracting my star athlete from getting her head in the game."

"No." Pete shrugged. "I am just here to cheer her on."

"How old are you?" Kurt asked, walking closer.

The two of them were almost at the same height. Pete was a little taller and broader in the shoulders.

"Nearly seventeen." Pete folded his arms. "How old are you?"

"Twenty-two. I have my degrees in exercise science, I live in my own apartment, and I passed the legal drinking age four years ago."

Pete chuckled. "You forgot to add your net worth and that you drive your own car."

"I was coming to that." Kurt squinted at him. "You are too involved with Giselle. I want you to back off."

"Hello, over here." Giselle got up and stood between the two of them. "Kurt, Pete is just a friend. Almost family. Let it go."

Pete was hopping mad after that. He didn't speak to her on the way to his choir practice. When she dropped him off, he glared at her. "Thank you for the lift 'almost' family."

"Pete, come on," Giselle pleaded, "you and I are just friends. We are not in a relationship."

"Just, friends?" Pete stepped back from the car. "You are still going with that fable?"

"It's not a fable." Giselle hissed. "There is nothing between us. We are not in a relationship. I don't love you."

Her voice hitched on the lie. "I don't feel anything for you but good old-fashioned friendship."

Pete laughed, dryly.

"You know what, Giselle? I wish I didn't love you so much. I wish that this thing for you would just leave me. I hate what you do to me. And you only do it because you have a giant chip on your shoulder about our age. Being nearly three years older is nothing, Giselle."

Giselle bit her lip, the word 'love' kept ringing in her ear. He loved her. She didn't want to admit, not even in her deepest private thoughts, that she felt the same way.

And the thought made her irritable. Maybe that was why she found herself snapping. "I think we shouldn't hang out so much. I think you should see other people. Maybe I will see Kurt, and you can see what's her name, Rylee."

"Fine." Pete snarled. "At least this time around, no one

will be hauling me off to a psychiatrist. See you around."

And just like that, a partial cold front descended on their relationship.

Giselle started dating Kurt, but her heart wasn't in it. She missed Pete. She followed his social media pages like a starving animal.

Kurt knew her heart wasn't in it either. She couldn't hide it from him. He knew she was pining after Pete. Their dates were mainly sport-centered. He was also car mad. And they talked about track a lot.

Even outside of training. There's wasn't the kind of relationship where she stayed up longer than she should to talk about music and books and inane stuff that other people would find boring, but she and Pete found engrossing.

And their first kiss was below par, maybe because she had the hot fiery kiss from Pete to compare it with. She was ready to say goodbye to Kurt after several months of thinking it was a bad idea to even start dating him.

She got the opportunity when she went to Kurt's mother's birthday party with him in late November. The track season was over, her exams were looming like a dark cloud, and Pete was on her mind.

Kurt's family was cool. They made much about her because she was the first girl that Kurt took to meet them. That gave her a pinch of fear. She didn't want to mean too much to Kurt.

His mother was a pretty Nigerian woman with a lilting accent that she hadn't lost even after being in Jamaica for thirty years. His father was a Korean man with a gentle smile. They were both Dr. Yu. His mother lectured at the University's medical school, and his father was a medical doctor with his own practice.

Giselle was a little overawed by Kurt's mother, she seemed

to have it all together. She was the kind of woman that Giselle envisioned that she would want to be like one day. And so it was almost disappointing when Dr. Yu took her aside and said to her, "I have been watching you and Kurt, and I must say it is obvious that he is more into you than you are into him. As a mother, I hate that. I don't expect you two to last. Let him down gently when you break up with him, please."

Giselle had not seen herself as some kind of femme fatale who broke men's hearts, but she was certainly placed in that situation by two parents so far. First Preston and now Dr. Yu.

She and Kurt had broken up shortly after that. He had caught her browsing through Pete's social media pictures before training.

"How often do you stalk him?" Kurt had asked over her shoulder.

Giselle jumped and closed her laptop. "Too often."

"What can I do to replace him in your thoughts in your mind in your affections?" Kurt asked exasperated.

"Nothing." Giselle had answered truthfully. "I just... Maybe we shouldn't see each other anymore. We should just go back to being just professional."

Kurt had looked at her, dispassionately. "That's it. You are done with our relationship?"

"That's right." Giselle nodded. "It's over."

"You are leaving me for Pete?" Kurt hissed. "The amazing Peter Wiley. What does that boy have, that has you so fixated?"

"I haven't seen him in months," Giselle muttered. "Last I heard he was dating Rylee Guthrie. They certainly seem to take a lot of pictures together."

Kurt laughed dryly. "Your jealousy is showing."

"I am not jealous of Pete," Giselle protested. "What's the matter with you?"

Kurt inhaled deeply and then shook his head. "I have never seen an intelligent woman be so blind. Anyway, he held up a finger before she protested. I always knew I was in Pete's shadow. I thought I could crawl out of it. I tried this past year."

Giselle turned her head away.

"I hope you are not going to let this affect us professionally," Kurt said. "I still think you are my star athlete."

Giselle nodded. "It will not."

"Good," Kurt murmured. "If I by any chance find myself a Rylee Guthrie, would you even care?"

"Oh, shut up." Giselle glared at him before going into her vehicle.

"That's what I thought." Kurt shook his head.

****

Giselle's twenty-first birthday rolled around with much fanfare. Toddy gave a speech at the breakfast table with a glimmer of a tear in his eye.

"Twenty-one is a significant milestone in our family."

Tiana looked at her watch, "Toddy I have a job interview at Cannon Publishers in forty minutes. This isn't going to be a long speech, is it?"

"You know what your problem is Tiana Pryce, you are not sentimental."

"I am," Tiana protested. "I also know that when you start off your speeches like this, you treat us like your audience in parliament."

"I am not boring or longwinded when I give speeches in the parliament," Toddy said gruffly.

"Depends on who you talk to," Elsa chuckled.

Giselle was half listening to them and thinking about how

she had ignored Pete's birthday party invitation. Nine days ago. He had texted her just this morning to tell her happy birthday. She felt bad about it because she had not told him a happy birthday on his day.

"Anyway," Toddy cleared his throat. "I was saying the reason why twenty-one is significant to us has a lot to do with our father. He made a duty of doing something special for us on that birthday. Since he is not here, I am going to continue the tradition."

Tiana cleared her throat.

"On my twenty-first birthday," Toddy was just getting warm, "I remember it clearly, we were sitting at the breakfast table, in a much humbler location than this. I had just graduated from university and was job hunting, and our father said, Jonathan Theodore Pryce, this is yours, he handed me an envelope and when I looked inside it was a cheque. Large enough for me to start my own business. I will never forget it."

Toddy reached behind him and handed them each a cheque. "I did it for all my children, I could afford to because of what Dad had done. And so, I bequeath unto you my lovely sisters the same thing, I stand in the gap for our dear father, Wilton Pryce, who is not here among the living. The cheque may not be as large as the one he gave me. Well, because there are three of you, and Mason Magnus is still at my coattails."

Giselle, Tiana, and Elsa had looked at each other with wide eyes. Giselle picked up her cheque gingerly and opened it. She squealed. "Toddy, this is amazing! Thank you!" She got up to hug him at the same time as Tiana and Elsa.

After the hugs, Toddy sighed. "I have other news."

"What is it, you are not sick, are you?" Elsa asked alarmed. "I have noticed that you are not acting yourself these days."

"No, I am not sick." Toddy sighed. "I am on the verge of

doing something that I vowed I would never do. I am selling the business. Pryceless Advertising is going belly up. I am just preempting its inevitable demise by off-loading it to the man who orchestrated its downfall."

"No." Giselle and Elsa gasped at the same time.

"Mason Magnus is bleeding me dry; he is expanding, and he offered me a price. My lawyers say it is good. I am going to sell it to him. Don't be sad about it, girls." Toddy smiled. "I spend more time playing golf these days than I do in the office, my seventieth birthday is quite near. I want a break. I have been thinking of downsizing my life for a while now."

"But I wanted a job at Pryceless after I graduated," Elsa moaned. "I mean, that is what I have been working toward. I wanted to make a name for myself in the advertising world."

"I know." Toddy nodded, "you are the only family member who cares about Pryceless, and I would have held on for you, but Mason is stealing all of my big clients. To be honest, I don't have the fight left in me to bother sparring with Mason. I still have my Senate seat at least. I can pay more attention to that. I am actually looking forward to it."

Tiana looked at the clock and then at Toddy. "Does this mean we are poor now?"

Toddy laughed. "No. We are scaling back, growing, moving on. I was hoping those cheques could help with each of you finding your own place. I want to sell this house. I already got an offer from a developer. I would move into something smaller. Maybe a three-bedroom townhouse or something."

"Oh for goodness sake," Elsa murmured, "this is not birthday news. You are selling the only home we have ever known, and you are selling the business I wanted to work at."

She grabbed her cheque and glared at Toddy. "I have to go to class. I have a presentation."

"I have to go to the interview." Tiana got up too and kissed him on the cheek. "Thanks again, Toddy."

Toddy watched them both walk away and then turned to Giselle.

"Why don't you look shocked at the latest developments?"

"Because it was only a matter of time before you downsized. This house is way too big for the five of us. I was looking forward to moving out, anyway."

Toddy nodded. "When I bought it, I had not anticipated the money pit it would be. Brandy had that child, who turned out not to be mine and then there were the three of you. I thought a big home was a good idea, but Brandy left and then there was just us and Myrna and whatever nanny was around at the time. It's only a matter of time before you three move out and then Myrna and I would be knocking about in here alone, and Myrna would be complaining about wanting to hire more people to keep it clean, plus I have to hire an army of landscapers to keep the grounds immaculate. Nobody tells you the costs of living in a pretty mansion, do they?"

Giselle nodded. "I understand totally. I just want to know how bad this whole takeover is. Are you really okay?"

"I am fine." Toddy patted her on the hand. "I have my health and my family. You know, Kaylon came first in his swimming competition last week?"

"Yes, I heard." Giselle smiled, but she figured everything was not all good as Toddy was saying. He would tell her what was bothering him in his own time.

Chapter Nine

Giselle was sitting in the sunken living room, psyching herself up to study. Weak sunlight poured through the floor to ceiling windows. The day couldn't make up its mind whether it wanted to be sunny or not.

She turned on the stereo and was too lazy to change the music from the music that Toddy had been listening to the night before in one of his rare downtime moments. Selling the business was wearing him out.

She looked into the ceiling and tried to picture Toddy without a business, a mansion, or his flashy cars, downsized and retired.

It was a little hard to picture. Toddy was a little like her or she was a little like Toddy since he was older. Driven.

What drove them was probably locked up somewhere in their genes. She looked across at the mantle place. There was a large black and white picture of their father, Wilton Pryce, and his first wife and all seven of their children, Toddy was in the middle with knee-high socks and shorts with suspenders.

All of them were driven people. There was a judge in there, a school principal, a couple of entrepreneurs, an ex-soldier turned inventor.

A few of them she had never met, well not until she had gotten that silver award at the World Championships. All of a sudden, the once cold and distant brothers and sisters and their offspring had wanted to be a part of her life.

She had suddenly become worthy of joining the club. How had her sister Caroline put it, she was definitely a Pryce.

Giselle had wanted to simultaneously laugh in her face and cry for that insensitive observation.

She had done neither.

In a way, her track and field career had brought the family together. There was nothing like a little fame and attention to have family members crawling out of the woodwork.

That was admittedly one of the reasons why she still pursued it. She craved the acceptance, the validation from the Pryce side of her family.

She closed her eyes tightly. No, she didn't.

Myrna's mumbo jumbo was getting to her.

"Hey you," Tiana said loudly over her head, "Giselle Amalia Pryce."

"Hey," Giselle opened her eyes.

Tiana grinned. "You were lost in thought."

"I was," Giselle nodded, "I have loads of things to think about."

"Have you thought about what you are going to do with your money?" Tiana sat across from her; she was still in her lucky red interview suit.

"I am going to buy myself a townhouse," Giselle said, "Jordan is building a townhouse complex near the Wiley Complex. It looks gorgeous. I want in. I have been secretly dreaming about it for a while."

Tiana raised an eyebrow. "That cheque cannot pay for a townhouse in the Wiley area."

"I know that." Giselle chuckled. "I am using some of my prize money, and I am getting a loan."

"Mmm." Tiana looked at her incredulously. "Do you know how much med school will cost? You should save your money for that."

"I applied for a scholarship." Giselle sat up and massaged her neck, "I think I will get it, my grades are perfect, my track record is healthy. I chose two schools that will find my athletics bent a bonus."

"Well then, a scholarship is the way to go about it because med school cost more than a house and it is time-consuming. You have to love it to pursue it. You sure that is what you want to do?"

"Why does everybody keep asking me that?" Giselle said exasperatedly. "I did Biology because I wanted to do medicine, I actually like it. I want to do Sports Medicine."

"I know," Tiana nodded. "You sure talk about it a lot but have you researched physiotherapy. I went to an interview today. My interviewer was in a wheelchair, and he was going on and on about his wonderful physiotherapist and how she was leaving Jamaica. The man was almost sobbing."

"Yeah, how did that go?" Giselle asked.

"I have no clue. I think Mr. Oliver, that's the interviewer's name, would have preferred if I had a Physiotherapist degree rather than one in English."

Giselle chuckled.

"Still, check it out," Tiana said, "There is a school in Florida that is accredited and all of that good stuff. You should apply to them."

"I know the one you are talking about, Groover College."

Giselle nodded, "my old Coach Stevens is working there now. He mentioned it in an email a year ago. I was hellbent on med school, so I dismissed it."

"Well, think about it," Tiana grinned. "Apply just in case you change your mind and apply for a scholarship too. You are going to need a scholarship if you spend all of your money on an apartment."

"I don't know," Giselle muttered.

"Tiana knows best." Tiana wagged her finger at her. "I am staying here until Toddy sells the place. I can't afford a house. Now I am feeling urgent about getting a job. You don't think Toddy is on the breadline, do you?"

"No," Giselle shook her head, "but he is worried about something. Knowing Toddy, he will not burden us with the nitty gritty as he likes to say."

"I know." Tiana sighed. "Now I wish that I did another degree. Why did I do English?"

"Because James Dalton had a lasting impact on you," Giselle murmured. "He was a good English teacher."

Tiana glared at her. "Anyway, moving on. I stopped by Waterfalls to have brunch with Sandrene after my disappointing interview. She sent over a birthday cake for the three of us. Three layers of, chocolate, strawberry, and vanilla."

"Sounds, yum." Giselle grinned, "I think I will have a piece. Then again, I may not. Sugar slows me down in training."

Tiana shook her head. "I couldn't do what you do. Don't get me wrong, I love your body, it is honed to perfection, but I just couldn't do the training."

"And that's fine." Giselle chuckled. "Nobody is asking you to."

"Anyway," Tiana clapped her hand eagerly, "I have to tell

you this, I saw someone today…"

"Who James Dalton?" Giselle grinned. "How is he these days? After you got him fired from the school, do you know what happened to him?"

"No. It's not James Dalton, and I don't know what he is up to." Tiana's voice dropped. "She glared at Giselle. When are you and everybody else in this family going to forget what I did?"

"Sorry." Giselle shrugged.

"I was talking about Pete." Tiana looked at her crossly. "You totally ruined the mood by bringing up James."

"Sorry," Giselle murmured. "Forgive me."

Tiana smirked. "I saw him today when I went to the Waterfalls. By the way, Sandrene said I could work there if this Editing job doesn't pan out..."

"How is he?" Giselle said quickly. "Who was he with?"

Tiana laughed and clapped her leg. "I am heartened Giselle that you are taking such an interest in my job offers."

Giselle glared at Tiana. "Pete, you were telling me about Pete."

"Pete is fine. Fabulous." Tiana mused. "He is all grown up. Tall and muscular and his voice is deeper and huskier. And he has that slow Wiley smile thing going on. He stares at you and then does a slow smile that seems to suck the air from around you and makes you want to check your makeup."

Giselle swallowed. "Really." Her voice came out in a squeak.

"Yes, honey child." Tiana grinned. "Sandrene said whenever Pete stops by all the girls in the building stop working. I can see why."

Giselle cleared her throat. "So he was there for Sandrene, not on a date?"

"There was this girl with him," Tiana said, watching her

sister eagerly. "She was hanging on to his every word."

Giselle sighed.

"But that didn't stop him from telling me to tell you…"

Giselle looked at her sharply. "What?"

"Give me your cheque and I'll tell you," Tiana teased.

"Haha, funny." Giselle glared at her sibling. "What did Pete say?"

"He said you should call him sometime." Tiana shrugged. "He said you should call him today; he has a surprise for you."

"I won't," Giselle said a stubborn tilt to her chin. "I am not going to be calling Peter Wiley."

"Okay." Tiana got up, "I am sure he is not short on calls. Anyway, I am going to get ready to go, I am going out with the girls. They have a party planned."

"Okay." Giselle nodded.

Tiana turned back and frowned at her. "You want me to stay with you? I know Elsa is celebrating with her friends. You have no one. You look so lonely. I could…"

"I am fine." Giselle grimaced. She hated feeling like the pathetic one with nobody to hang with on her birthday. Georgia was in mommy mode; she had no time for her. She would have been Giselle's first port of call if she weren't otherwise occupied.

She picked up her cell phone as soon as Tiana left the room. That last statement did her in. She was not lonely. She was fine. She didn't mind her own company, and she did need to get ahead with the studying for this year. This was her last semester. She would celebrate when it was over.

She didn't know why she was dialing Pete's number. She wouldn't let it ring more than two times. She had much better things to do than to be calling Pete.

It rang once, and he answered.

"Hey," Pete said casually as if they were still on speaking terms, and they hadn't had a year of no contact.

Giselle cleared her throat. "Hey."

"Happy birthday," Pete said. "There was a smile in his voice. I have been waiting on this call."

"Thank you for the birthday wishes. I don't know why I called." Giselle grumbled.

"I have your present," Pete said, "do you want it this evening or…"

"I never expected that you would remember my birthday," Giselle laughed uncomfortably, "and I had no intentions of going out. I was planning to study."

"It's your twenty-first birthday," Pete said jovially, "surely you could put the books down for a minute. We could go to Strawberry Hills. I have a spa reservation for one Giselle Pryce."

"The spa? You have a reservation?" Giselle asked.

"Yes," Pete said. "If you hadn't called, I would have called you. Are you still pretending that you are seeing Kurt?"

"No." Giselle felt compelled to answer. "I wasn't pretending. We broke up some weeks back. Who was that girl Tiana saw you with today?"

"Laura," Pete chuckled. "I gave her a ride to work. She works close to the Waterfalls. She likes me, but I told her about you."

"About me?" Giselle sat up straighter in her chair, "what do you mean?"

"I told her that you were my girl," Pete said without a hint of mirth. "I told her when you called me later, we would be back on again."

"We were never off." Giselle said heatedly, "because we were never on. You are so sure of yourself when it comes to me, it is frightening and a little cocky."

Pete laughed. "Cocky as in self-assured, confident? You may be right. Do you want me to come and pick you up at three? It should be a nice drive up to Irish Town."

"I don't want to go anywhere," Giselle grumbled.

Pete laughed again. "See you in a bit."

****

He arrived a half hour later. She had showered put on a white strapless dress that showed off her every curve. Tiana saw her heading downstairs and whistled.

"Wow." Tiana chuckled. "You are looking like a hot meal. How can I be as hot as you, Giselle Wiley?"

Giselle glared at her. "Train six days a week. And why are you calling me Giselle Wiley?"

"I am a prophetess." Tiana grinned. "They call me Madam Tiana."

"Madam Tiana, you are way off." Giselle laughed and headed to the door. Pete was standing there, the sunlight streaming behind him. She blinked a little because she had to look up at him. He smelled so good; she was leaning forward to get a whiff.

"Hey, I forgot to tell you happy new year too." Pete smiled. "I think this is going to be a good year."

Giselle nodded. It certainly felt like it was going to be a good year with him standing there.

"Happy new year to you too and happy belated birthday." She smiled, "I am going to get my shoes. Want to come inside? Madam Tiana is prophesying."

Pete chuckled.

Tiana was standing on the landing of the stairs. "Hi, Pete. Doesn't Gis look good in white?"

"She does," Pete said, "I was going to tell her, but I didn't want to spook her. Giselle gets weird over compliments."

Tiana laughed. "I predict that she will be Giselle Wiley by next year."

"Stop it." Giselle hissed to Tiana.

She glanced at Pete though to gauge his reaction, and their eyes met.

He wasn't laughing. He stared at her solemnly. "I wouldn't mind."

Giselle didn't know why she felt so weak in the knees after that or why she felt like her feet had difficulty moving one before the other when she went into her room and her shoe closet. She chose a white wedge heel to match her outfit, and looked in the closet for a throw, she knew how chilly Irish Town could get in January. She also took her hair out of its single plait. Pete liked it when it was down.

A pair of hoops and some lip gloss and she grabbed her bag. She looked good. Her dusky complexion against the white dress was striking. She needed to wear dresses more often.

She didn't want to think about Tiana's insinuations about marriage to Pete. That was something that was far in her future if it would even happen.

****

Pete went all out for the date. Her present was a full spa treatment.

"Because you need to relax," he told her teasingly. "Your dinner awaits when you are done. I have a studio cottage. It's a private party."

Giselle stared at him bemusedly as he walked away and left her to the smiling spa staff.

"You are a lucky girl." One of the attendants said to her

grinning.

"Apparently, I am." Giselle giggled. She felt lighthearted and curiously settled in her mind. She had never gotten a full spa treatment before, and the staff spoiled her.

When she exited the spa area and headed to the cottage, she felt waxed and polished and weightless.

The cottage was surrounded by foliage and had a view of Kingston in the distance. The table on the balcony was set. The four-poster bed in the middle of the room was surrounded by drapes. The jalousies and fretwork on the cottage let in the weak evening light.

She heard music. Soft and low. Reggae love songs. Her favorites.

Pete was waiting for her on the veranda. He had his tablet with him, playing her favorites. He had come prepared to impress.

"How do you feel?" He asked, smiling at her as she stood at the balcony and looked over at the view in the setting sun.

"Like this is a fairy tale." Giselle looked at him accusingly, "I told you this was a fantasy of mine to stay here and to eat under the stars. This is a fantasy brought to life."

Pete smiled. "I remembered every detail."

"You are seducing me, Pete," Giselle said. "I am not sure that I want to be seduced. It is not in my plans."

He got up and stood beside her curving his fingers around hers. "Is that a bad thing?"

"It's not what I want right now." Giselle looked at him with all the pent-up emotions she had inside for him. "We shouldn't be alone like this. We create sparks off each other. I don't want a relationship."

"I know." Pete moved closer to her, "and yet here we are. Dinner will be served in half an hour. After we eat, we can leave."

They ate on the veranda. The food was good. She didn't eat much of it though. She kept staring at Pete and he at her.

If looks could spark theirs would catch fire.

After dinner and the dishes were cleared away by silent discrete staff, they looked at each other across the flickering lamplight.

Giselle who was not given to flights of fantasy, nor was she used to throwing caution to the wind, thought about doing just that. What would it be like to finally give in to her desire for Pete?

She didn't have to ask he wanted her too. It was at that moment the song, Woman came on. The reggae cover by Peter Lloyd.

Pete got up and held out his hands. She went into his arms like a homing pigeon. They danced slowly to the music while Pete serenaded her.

And woman hold me close to your heart... I love you now and forever...

That was it. The song that broke down every one of her defenses. She was the one who kissed him first.

Chapter Ten

A knock on her car window dragged Giselle back to the present in a rush. She wound her car window down. It was Elsa. As usual, Elsa was looking stunning. This morning she was in a tight black pencil skirt that enhanced her slim figure and a red blouse with a bow at the neck. She looked like she stepped off the cover of a business magazine. Her lip color matched her blouse. She had gotten a job at a small advertising firm just a few weeks before, and she was dressing like a fashion plate ever since.

She had a briefcase in one hand and a net with some balls in the other.

"What are you doing here, Gis?" Elsa asked frowning. "Why do I sense that you are in distress?"

"I am pregnant," Giselle said emotionlessly, "and I am thinking of abortion, for my career sake. I had planned to do it in secret and not to tell anyone. And here I am just blurting it out to you. I know all the arguments to keep it and all the arguments why I can't. At this point, I don't even think I care about any great debate. I just want my life back to how it was before."

Elsa's mouth formed in an o and then she opened the car door. "Come here, what you need is a hug."

Giselle stepped into her sister's perfumed arms and started to cry.

They stood there for what seemed like hours, and then Giselle felt Tiana behind her, and she was shuttled to another shoulder where she started crying afresh.

"I am a bad person." She howled. "I hate myself for thinking about the easy way out. I hate myself for lying to Pete. I told him that this was Kurt's baby and he left last night. He hates me now. He probably thinks I am the scum of the earth."

Elsa rubbed her back while Tiana whispered in her ear. "It will be all right. You'll see."

She was a mess when she finally leaned on the car and looked at her sisters.

They were dressed for work. They looked immaculate; their lives were going in the trajectory where they both wanted. While hers was in disarray.

"A baby is a blessing," Elsa said. "I won't try to influence you one way or the other because I know you will make the right choice for yourself eventually. And I know this because I know you. I have to confess. I can't help but feel a little excited about becoming an aunt. The news is growing on me."

"Me too." Tiana smiled. "Oh, goodness, I am going to be an aunt. I hope it's a girl. If it's a boy, no problem but a girl… we can go shopping together and play with makeup."

"What about my career and my life?" Giselle asked. "You guys are not getting it."

"At the end of the day," Elsa raised an eyebrow, "can a career hug you and call you Mommy?"

"Besides, I know lots of athletes who become mothers and then compete." Tiana cleared her throat, "so who is the dad?"

"No comment," Giselle said hoarsely. "I shouldn't have dragged him into this. I ruined his life. I told him this was not his baby anyway. I am going this alone."

"That's foolish." Tiana scoffed. "Tell us who it is."

"No." Giselle shook her head. "It won't matter in the long run. I don't want someone staking a claim on my body and telling me what to do. I can't tell you because I don't want him to know."

Tiana and Elsa looked at each other meaningfully.

"Okay," Elsa finally said, "keep your secret. If it's Kurt's the Korean will show, and then it won't be a secret anymore."

Giselle looked from one sister to the other.

"Exercise good judgment in this, Gis. Please," Tiana said earnestly. "Remember, we are here for you. You have support."

Elsa nodded firmly. "You should move back in."

"No thanks," Giselle muttered. "Isn't Toddy going to be selling this place soon. I am going to make you guys late for work."

"Work can wait." Elsa shrugged. "If you want, I can spend today with you. Are you going to tell Toddy now?"

"I don't know." Giselle sighed. "I still don't know what I am going to do. I think I want to be alone today to think this through."

Elsa inhaled loudly. "Okay. Call me later?"

Giselle nodded.

Tiana gave her a brief hug and then looked at her solemnly. "You are strong. You will handle motherhood like a boss."

When they left Giselle got in her car. She didn't have the

energy for Toddy and Myrna. She would go home, turn off her phone, and vegetate just for today.

****

Unfortunately, meditation was off the books for her when she went home. Pete was lounging in her living room when she got there. She wished she hadn't given him his own keys.

He looked a little worse for wear as if he hadn't slept the night before. Giselle got a glimpse of herself in the hallway mirror. She didn't look much better.

"Hey," she whispered her voice hoarse.

"Hey," Pete said lazily. "You must have left here at the crack of dawn."

"Yes, went to the track club," Giselle sat across from Pete.

"To tell Kurt about the baby?" His voice cracked at baby. And that's when she realized that Pete was not as calm as he appeared.

She sighed. "I went to see a friend to get the name of her doctor. She had an abortion last year."

Pete closed his eyes and swallowed. "Gis…"

"I can't believe you called Kurt," Giselle said heatedly. "What's the matter with you? I didn't want anybody to know. This was supposed to be easy and private. Nobody had to know about this. You, Kurt, nobody!"

"I know that is what you want, but I know that you are not thinking straight." Pete opened his eyes. "I went home last night, livid. Absolutely livid. I felt betrayed, I felt loss, I felt as if you stabbed me in the back."

Giselle frowned. "And you told your parents."

"No, just my dad." Pete shrugged. "I am sure he has told my mom by now."

"I am too tired to care that you tell Preston everything."

Giselle sighed. "He is your father, not your best friend or priest. Why are you two so close?"

Pete smiled, sadly. "I love having him as a friend. Do you know how many boys wish they had the kind of relationship with their father that I have with mine? That's why I'll make a good father. I think, I have a great example."

"I know you would be a great father. I just…" Giselle bit her lip. "I am selfish. I am only thinking about what I want in this situation. I just…," She swallowed. "I want to just chew this over for a while alone."

Pete inhaled and then exhaled loudly. "Giselle, somebody has to fight for that baby's right to live. I decided to appoint myself as the one to do it."

"Whether you are the father or not?" Giselle asked sharply. "What's wrong with you?"

"You are what's wrong with me," Pete said snidely. "I have always thought that somehow, we could work but you can't be selfish in relationships. Putting us aside, there is a life at stake here."

"Can we please not talk about any of this today?" Giselle asked after Pete's outburst.

"I wouldn't mind not talking about it for the next eight months," Pete murmured. "We can just sit here and let things take their natural course."

"And then I'd have the baby." Giselle got up and started pacing. "Pete, I am not ready to be a mother. This whole thing is scary."

"I know." Pete nodded. "It is new, it is out of our comfort zone. It scares me, too, but I don't want to take the easy way out."

"If this is your kid, don't you understand how much this will change your life?" Giselle asked, widening her eyes. "You are in your first year at university."

"Taking courses that are too easy for me." Pete shrugged. "I can handle this, Gis. I already make money. I have a couple top app earners. I even got an offer the other day to develop an app for a bank. Rylee's father saw an app we were working on, and he want us to do one for his company. What they are paying for it is pretty impressive."

"Rylee," Giselle made a face. "How is she these days?"

"Good," Pete frowned. "Still pretty and charming and smart."

"Bleh," Giselle made a face.

Pete didn't respond.

"She'll be devastated that I am pregnant," Giselle murmured, "not only her, your church sisters are going to be disappointed. They'll ban you from the choir. If the baby is yours."

Pete winced.

She was laying it on thick, pushing him away and she couldn't help herself. Giselle folded her arms as if she were cold. "Everyone will know that you are not their perfect little choir boy if I have the baby."

Pete laughed. "I haven't been the perfect choir boy for months. I can live with the disappointment. It is much preferable than you not having the baby."

"If this baby is yours, I am not going to get married to make this pregnancy palatable to your church members either," Giselle mumbled.

"Nobody said anything about marriage we were not even in a relationship, remember," Pete got up. "When I marry anyone, it will be because she wants me more than she wants her career. I am not interested in taking back seat to anything in her life. The same would go for me too, she would always come first. Front seat all the way, without that, I am not interested in marriage."

"You sound so certain," Giselle said faintly, "life is not so simple."

"It might not be," Pete headed to the door, "but let me tell you it is nowhere as complicated as you are making it out to be."

Giselle felt the tears as they gathered at the corners of her eyes.

Pete was looking at her with contempt. She felt like confessing the truth about her and Kurt, She felt like walking over to him and hugging him and confess that she was lying. Kurt was not in the picture; he was her first and her only lover.

But now was the time to end what they had, Pete would not forgive her for the abortion if she had it, and she couldn't live with his recriminations and her own guilt.

He had his hand on the door, his back to her.

"I don't want to see you again, Pete, whatever we had is over." She cleared her throat; the delivery was too husky and a little needy. She drummed up her coldest, frostiest voice. "What is happening to me is none of your business."

Pete turned around and looked at her for so long Giselle was on the verge of squirming.

"Okay," he said quietly, "if that is what you want."

He fished out her key from his pocket and placed it on the table beside the door and left.

She heard the door click, and it felt so final. Her heart was beating in a weird trippy way, and she felt like running outside and begging him to give her time to make up her mind where she wanted to go with this and not leave her.

Instead, she sat on the sofa and sobbed— choking, wailing, sobs that wouldn't stop.

What had she done?

Chapter Eleven

Time had a way of plodding by when one was laboring under life-changing decisions and a broken heart of her own making. She read through the fine print of both her scholarship offers. She had gotten them based on merit rather than need.

That meant that her grades were the reason she was considered more than her financial situation. Maybe just maybe that would mean that she would still qualify, but under the eligibility criteria, there was the wording for both scholarship offers.

Scholarships will be revoked if student is convicted of a felony conviction, repeated illegal use of narcotics, including marijuana or controlled substances, failure to comply with the rules and regulations of the college, or the athletic team or activity of which the student is a member, failure to cooperate with officials and instructors at the college.

It didn't say pregnancy.

Giselle inhaled raggedly. Maybe she still had a chance.

She called both schools. And asked if she could still get a scholarship if she were pregnant. Oh no, was the reply.

Can I defer the scholarship to another year? One of the ladies she spoke to had laughed, medical school scholarships are scarce. Acceptance is in three weeks; one had reminded her a hint of censure in her tones.

It was as if the lady was marveling at her stupidity to actually get pregnant and give up such a golden opportunity.

Giselle paced the house, feverishly thinking. Med school was expensive. It was normally expensive, for an International student it was even worse. It would take her four years to finish med school, and three to five years of residency. She wanted to do sports medicine, that would include a two-year fellowship. That was nine years out of her life. Nine!

Her doorbell sounded, and she stopped pacing long enough to drag it open without looking in the peephole.

"Hey, I brought you something to eat and groceries." It was Pete, a solemn Pete, with bags of groceries in his arms. She couldn't contain her joy.

"Oh, hey," Giselle swallowed. "You… ah, you are here."

"I am a sucker for punishment," Pete said, "yesterday was emotionally charged, and we were both not thinking rationally. It can't be a final goodbye between us until I am sure one way or the other about what you are going to do about…" his wandered down to her still flat stomach, "the baby."

Giselle nodded. "I appreciate the groceries and the food I haven't eaten all day. What did you get?"

"Something from the Waterfall. I designed an app for them so Sandrene is very grateful. I get periodic food perks."

Giselle opened the box with the food and inhaled. "This smells so good. What is it?"

"Grilled Oriental Chicken Salad." Pete looked at her, wearily. "You can't be skipping meals, Gis. You have someone else to think of now."

"I know." Giselle started eating. It was a lot of salad, and it tasted as good as it looked. "So I called the universities today, and I am not eligible for the scholarships if I am pregnant and I was just here pacing and thinking why do I want to do medicine? It is nine years out of my life. I did four years of bio already, that would be thirteen.

"I can't afford this, Pete. I mean not only financially but time wise. Coupled with that, I would have to train like a beast, I compete in one of the most competitive events, the four hundred meters."

Pete watched her as she spoke. He could never get tired of watching Giselle. He currently disliked her strongly, but he would never not love her.

"So, what are you going to do?"

"I could be a physiotherapist instead. It's just two years of my life after this." Giselle made a face. "That's my ex-coaches' specialty, you know. He wanted me to come with him a couple of years ago. Tiana convinced me to apply to his school, I haven't heard from them yet."

"You are still pregnant." Pete pointed out.

"Yes, there is that." Giselle sighed. "I am still thinking about what to do about my er condition."

"You need to do the right thing," Pete repeated, sounding like a broken record.

"And the right thing in your eyes is to have this baby and give up on my dreams and plans." Giselle grimaced.

"You don't have to give up on your dreams," Pete said gently, "you can give the baby to me and then go follow your dreams."

"Give the baby to you." Giselle raised an eyebrow, "do

you realize that you are only eighteen?"

"Nineteen in a couple of months." Pete reminded her bitingly. "And I am more than mature enough to manage fatherhood. Please bear that in mind before you make up excuses for me."

"My scholarships…" Giselle said mournfully.

Pete's phone rang before he could say anything else. "Hey, Rylee."

Of course, it had to be Rylee.

Rylee with the pretty face and the killer body and the brain of a machine. She was the total package. She was a genius. A certified genius just like Guy. They belonged to the same chapter of MENSA.

At least Rylee had sense enough not to get pregnant when she had her whole life ahead of her.

Giselle made a face. Pete spent a good while going over some design or the other with her, talking computer code language.

He went for his computer and was so engrossed in his conversation; she felt a little resentful. She watched as his fingers flew over the keys. Was he even ready to be a father? He was so engrossed in what he was talking about with Rylee, he had forgotten she was there.

"Got it, sending it to you," he said, "give me your feedback."

He looked up at her scowling face when he got off the phone. "Where were we?

"I was thinking that you were not ready for fatherhood," Giselle smirked.

"And I was saying that it doesn't matter if you think I am ready. It is fait accompli, already done. I'll learn, I'll adjust, I'll cope."

"Have you ever kissed Rylee?" The thought came to her.

"Weren't you two an item one time?"

"You mean in the year that you ditched me?" Pete asked. "Yes, I've kissed her. Yes, we were an item and…"

"And?" Giselle growled a pinprick of jealousy had her in its grip.

"And?" Pete smiled slowly.

"Have you gone further?" Giselle glared at him.

"No sex," Pete said. "Unlike you, I don't have multiple sexual partners."

"I don't either," Giselle snapped. "You know I didn't."

"Well, just yesterday, you told me this was Kurt's kid." Pete pointed out cruelly.

"I said it could be," Giselle said weakly. "Could be, is not definite. Could be, means that you don't go announcing this to all your family and no one will pressure me to have this baby. I have to make up my mind."

"When the baby is born and doesn't look Korean," Pete said, "all doubts will be laid to rest."

"If I have this baby, Giselle said pointedly. "If… if… if…

"If you have this baby," Pete repeated. "I hate the word if."

"And if I have this baby and it turns out to be yours, I don't want Rylee playing stepmother in his life."

"You never know what can happen in life," Pete said cryptically. "Look at us. I thought we would be together forever, but I don't factor in your plans. I am kind of sick of it."

"I don't want to fight." Giselle shook her head. "I have other things to think about."

"As usual, I am not in the forefront of your thoughts." Pete walked over to her and wrapped his hand around her hair, his favorite gesture. "Whenever you and I make love it's the only time I have your undivided attention. That's the only time I am the center of your universe when you are writhing under me and begging for more."

"Pete…"

"It's true," Pete said. "I approach this relationship unselfishly and with love. I would do anything for you while you just use me. I am surplus to requirements. Just like the baby. You need to hear the truth, Giselle. You are a user who wants to kill my child."

Giselle gasped.

He looked at her dispassionately.

"Let me know what you decide about the baby. I am not too interested in hearing you moan about your precious scholarship and your precious career for a minute more."

"Are you leaving?" Giselle whispered when he started packing up his computer and shoving it into his bag aggressively.

"Yup." Pete nodded, "being around you makes me anxious and mad. This is torture. You are right, the scales have fallen from my eyes. I am going to be staying far, far from you after this."

He left before she could refute what he said. She wasn't using him or torturing him. She had to decide what was best for her future. She couldn't throw all her goals away on a relationship that might not even last. They had one glaring thing in common, an intense attraction to each other. She was waiting for it to burn out. That it had only gotten stronger through the years was irrelevant. It would burn out one day.

And yes, she enjoyed sex with him. She hadn't foreseen that she would. Pete was an unselfish lover and person in general.

She always knew she was going to go away to med school. She always knew that their futures were not on a collision course, they would take diverging roads. They were very different people.

This baby was not planned.

She sighed and cupped her chin. This was just another point of contention to worry about, she couldn't think about Pete and his assumptions right now. She had a lot more things to worry about.

****

Coach Stevens was happy to talk to her when she called the next day. He had always been a sympathetic listener.

When she mentioned the scholarships, he was heartwarmingly excited for her, and when she told him, she had applied to his school. He was beyond ecstatic.

"Yes!" He squealed with delight. "You'll love it here. The physiotherapy program is world class."

Then she told him she was pregnant, and he paused so long she wondered if he was still on the phone.

"How pregnant are you?" He asked disappointment in his voice.

Giselle told him. She knew the exact date of her conception.

"Then you'll give birth by April/May. Rest up for a couple of weeks and be in training by July/August," he said, sounding optimistic again.

"Your grades are perfect; you'll get your acceptance letter soon. As for scholarships, I don't know if you'll be offered one for next year. I have never heard of a pregnant student getting one. You can always apply for the year after."

Giselle exhaled. "Okay."

She would have to crunch numbers. She hadn't planned on financing a master's degree and having a baby. She had drained her account when she bought the apartment and furnished it. She had fixed investments that she couldn't touch without penalty. She was in a bind.

Her sponsorships would go away if she had the baby. Everybody wanted to sponsor a winning athlete, a practicing athlete, not one on a break or one who was bouncing back. And it would take her a while to bounce back.

She wasn't going to ask her relatives for money. It was out of the question. She was too independent for that. And frankly had too much pride. The easiest solution would be to just have the abortion. The pros were looking much better than the cons.

She pulled on her tracksuit and went for a walk to clear her mind. She wasn't in panic mode anymore; she had a lot of scenarios to think through.

She walked through her residential neighborhood and further up the road to where Georgia lived. It was a spur of the moment thing. She didn't even know if Georgia was home from work. They hadn't been keeping in touch as much as they used to lately.

She dialed her number, and Georgia answered brightly, "Hey best friend."

"I am outside," Giselle said.

"Yes!" Georgia chortled. "I am home, just got in. We can share some mimosas and pretend that we are young again."

Giselle giggled. "Okay old lady, let me in."

Chapter Twelve

"**F**inally, we meet again, best friend," Georgia plopped herself down in front of Giselle. "It has been months. The phone calls are not the same. Sometimes I need to look in your face when we talk."

"I know," Giselle said brightly.

"You can't fool me, something is wrong; your eyes are sad." Giselle sat down in one of Georgia's overstuffed couches and sighed. "You got me."

Georgia had gained a lot of weight over the years since she quit track and field and after her pregnancy with Nyla. She was practically bursting out of her blue work suit.

"One mimosa coming up." Georgia headed to her open plan kitchen.

"No alcohol for me, just juice," Giselle said, she read somewhere that pregnant women were not supposed to be drinking alcohol.

Georgia spun around dramatically. "What? Why? You've

gone teetotal on me? I thought this was the offseason."

"There is no offseason with Kurt Yu as the head of Velocity. Giselle grinned. "Besides, I am not drinking because... eye roll please…"

Georgia obliged, rolling her eyes comically.

"I am pregnant."

Georgia sat on the floor. Giselle heard her skirt make a ripping sound.

"Drat it," Georgia murmured, "My skirt is split all the way to the belt."

Giselle laughed.

"Pregnant." Georgia said slowly, "which would mean you are having sex. Sex without marriage. I thought you said, you would not be having sex outside of marriage and that I was stupid for getting pregnant when I did."

"I didn't say stupid." Giselle corrected her, "I would never say that."

"That must have been my inner voice," Georgia murmured. "The critical one does sound a lot like you."

"It does? How appalling." Giselle frowned. "I am not that bad. I am not a critic."

"I don't make the voices, they just form in my head, I have a snooty one that sounds like my sister, Malia," Georgia said. "So whose kid is it?"

"Pete." Giselle watched as Georgia digested that bit of information.

"You finally gave in to your lust for Pete." Georgia grinned. "You've been hankering for that boy since he was a tot."

"He was not a tot." Giselle sighed. "I don't know why I even told you, I don't know if I'll have the baby."

"Say what?" Georgia widened her eyes. "Abortion! The big A! For heaven's sake, you won't be able to live with yourself if you do it."

"I don't know." Giselle massaged her neck. "I can't get my scholarships if I am pregnant."

"Scholarships? As in two?" Georgia widened her eyes dramatically.

"Yep." Giselle nodded. "Ivy league schools too."

"Some girls have all the luck," Georgia started singing sadly, "some girls have all the luck, some girls have all the pain, Some girls get all the breaks, some girls do nothing but complain…"

"Shut up," Giselle threw a pillow at Georgia. "Haven't you heard a word I said. I am pregnant. If I have this baby, it means no scholarship for either school. I spent all of the money that Toddy gave me earlier this year along with some of my savings on my apartment."

"I see." Georgia got up and headed to the kitchen. "I think I need the mimosa. I can better guide you when I am fortified with the juice of life."

"You are turning into a drunk. Where is Nyla?"

"With Calvin's parents for the week. They love her to bits. Too bad their son is a deadbeat dad, who recently got another girl pregnant. Nyla is going to be a big sister."

"Oh," Giselle nodded. "Sorry to hear."

"I am long past caring." Georgia shrugged. "I made a huge mistake with him."

"Pete doesn't want me to have the abortion," Giselle said. "He said he would take the baby and let me go ahead and fulfill my dreams. He doesn't even know if the kid is his. I lied to him told him it could be Kurt's."

"As in Kurt Yu?" Georgia widened her eyes, "what are you getting up to?"

"Nothing. Never slept with Kurt."

"Oh," Georgia said in relief. "I know your leopard did not change its spots so thoroughly."

"I should have hooked up with Pete," Georgia murmured. "I wouldn't be a single parent with a whore of an ex-boyfriend if I did, but then again, I wouldn't have stood a chance, Pete has always been singularly focused on you. Do you want orange juice?"

"Thank you," Giselle said contemplatively.

"I would hold on to Pete if I were you," Georgia said, putting much more champagne in her glass than was necessary. "He is a keeper."

"You think we would last? I mean," Giselle took the orange juice from Georgia, "everybody eventually breaks up. This dating world is dismal."

"It is dismal because of us women. We choose the wrong men, immature babies who have no sense. We choose them based on looks as if how a person's features are arranged can feed you when you are hungry or hug you when you are down, and we don't insist on commitment before sex, and I mean serious commitment like marriage.

"That way if he has the slightest inclination to wonder he will think twice because he knows you will ruin his bank account and you'll take the house.

Giselle burst out laughing. "Amen."

"We have one-night stands, and we mix men, and we don't know who our baby daddies are because we don't respect ourselves and then we bring babies into this world, and the cycle continues. Women can change the dating game easily."

"All of that on just one sip of a mimosa?" Giselle giggled.

"There is more." Georgia held up her fingers, "I am an expert at this. Many sleepless nights have put things into perspective for me."

She took a big gulp and drained her glass. "Let me tell you, motherhood without support is no walk in the park. The other night when Nyla was teething and bawling her head off in the complex, I knew my neighbors were cursing me silently. I got a few looks in the morning. Listen, it was so bad, I sat with her in my lap in the living room and bawled with her. I felt so overwhelmed. The child does not sleep at nights, and I have to work for a living. While I was bawling, I wished that I was a trophy wife with a rich husband and several nannies at my beck and call."

Giselle smiled.

"And don't let me get started on the ruination of my shape." Georgia got up. The gap in her skirt was gawping even wider. "Even though I don't think you'll have to worry about that Miss Athlete, but I can't find the time to go to the gym or comb my hair or get a mani/pedi. And the basic things that I used to find so important, like going clubbing and hanging with friends can't fit into my life. Nyla is my whole world. It is laughable that you think that you can just have the kid and then hand it off to Pete and then seamlessly go back to just being Giselle. You will be a mommy. A mommy has different priorities."

Giselle shrugged. "I think I can do it."

Georgia laughed. "You know what, I should have taped this conversation. You are going to be singing a different tune soon. Your world will change, your priorities will shift."

"So you are saying I should have the abortion?" Giselle asked.

"Oh no," Georgia shook her head, "no. I think you should have the child, if anybody can pull off a comeback, it's you. You have the single-minded determination for that. Have the child and then give it to Pete as he requested. He has no idea what he is getting himself into, but what the hey, women have been pacing the floor at nights for years. You didn't get pregnant by yourself."

"And you don't think I am absolutely horrible for

contemplating abortion?" Giselle asked.

"No, not horrible." Georgia shook her head. "I would think you are horrible if you went through with it. You would go down a notch in my estimation, knocked off the pedestal I have you on."

Giselle chuckled. "You mean I am not knocked off yet? I am an unmarried mother to be."

"Join the club. Stuff happens." Georgia shrugged. "Condoms break, morning after pills fail, the only way to be certain you won't be in this situation is to remain celibate. I went to a church lecture once the presenter said, 'be happy in your singleness. Bask in your drama free life.' I thought she was spouting crap and wasn't getting any. And so, here I am, wishing I had her life."

Giselle laughed. She needed to hang out with Georgia more. She had forgotten what a breath of fresh air she was in her life.

"What I wouldn't do to bask in some drama free life." Georgia drained her glass. "These things finish too fast."

"Elsa and Tiana are celibate," Giselle murmured. "I am the only non-celibate triplet."

"Lies," Georgia giggled. "I can kind of see Tiana being a virgin but not Elsa. Elsa is the wild fun version of you. Tell me, how can the fun version of you be a virgin and the boring version of you be a sexually liberated millennial?"

"Is that a nice way of saying slut?" Giselle raised her eyebrows.

"Slut, no." Georgia pretended to clutch her pearls. "I would never say that. I am a fellow sexually liberated millennial. I think the word slut is offensive. How often do you do it with Pete?"

"Since we started?" Giselle raised her eyebrows, "every day. We didn't go all the way until a couple of weeks ago. I was all over Europe this summer for the Diamond League. I came back for Case's wedding, and then there was the night after the wedding, and we had this little fantasy…"

"Slut," Georgia laughed.

Giselle grimaced. "I love being intimate with Pete. The first time was the first time for both of us, and it was off the charts crazy. Like fireworks and chocolate crazy. Pete is not a selfish lover; I can tell you that."

Georgia shook her head. "My first time was off the charts lousy. I shouldn't have done it again. The second time was even worse than the first. And I went back for a third and a fourth. All lousy. I am going to have to find me a Pete. All in the confines of marriage and financial stability, of course."

Giselle chuckled. "Of course. More juice please, I am running out."

She looked at Georgia fondly as she went back to the kitchen, "I am happy I came over to talk to you."

"Me too," Georgia grinned. She fixed another glass of mimosa for herself. "Will you look at the two of us? This is not how we planned our lives, was it?"

"No. Giselle sighed. "But in the words of Elsa Pryce the fun version of me, plans are not set in stone, and stuff happens, so suck it up bunny."

"Suck it up, bunny." Georgia clinked her glass to hers.

****

One week later, Giselle had still not made up her mind about what she was going to do. The panic had left. The news was slowly growing on her. She still didn't leave the house for close to a week. She only answered calls from her sisters.

And on Tuesday when they called and said that Toddy had

sold the house, she wished she hadn't answered. Even though she didn't live there anymore, she fell into a depressive state when she got the news.

She felt as if the changes were coming at her too rapidly for her to keep up. There were barely any anchors left for her to cling to.

Her life had taken a nosedive in the wrong direction. One minute she was Giselle Pryce athlete on the rise, a top scholar with two scholarships, the next she was a washed-up wannabe. Pregnant with no boyfriend.

After a week of no contact, she showed up for training an hour later than usual. Except for Amara the lounge was empty. It was her time slot. Giselle glanced at the roster; her name was not on it.

Amara looked at her quizzically. "How did it go?"

"I er, I don't know. I didn't go through with it."

Amara nodded. "Well don't."

Giselle sat down with her backpack at her feet. "I don't know about that."

Amara shrugged. "For a smart girl you really messed up big time, didn't you?"

That was uncalled for and pretty cold. Giselle protested in her head. And more accurate than she cared to admit.

She watched as Amara exited the lounge and then she swung around and stared at the television blankly. What was she doing?

It was a travesty to even attempt to train. This morning she had mild morning sickness. Nothing too heavy. Just a little dizziness if she jumped out of bed too suddenly. She couldn't even think of hurdling right now. She was more prone to hurling than hurdling. The joke rang in her head, and she dismissed it. This was no joke.

She had to apply for sick leave. Unfortunately, applying

for sick leave was involved getting a note from her doctor. She got up, headed to her car, and called her GP. Anthea Stevens. Anthea started work pretty early. She was the club's official doctor and pretty much the only one they accepted a sick leave from. Giselle had no need to see anyone else through the years.

"Meet me at the office in twenty," Anthea said cheerfully.

Giselle groaned; Anthea had recently moved to the what was loosely called Wiley Complex Two. It was beside the original Wiley Complex; it was smaller and mostly had medical-related businesses on there.

It was not a given that she would meet any of the Wileys. She had to assume that Pete had not said anything further to Preston or any of the others because no one had shown up at her apartment with a shotgun in hand telling her to repent and to admit the truth to Pete.

It was really over between them. She hadn't heard a word from Pete either.

She scrolled through his social media pages. There was a picture of him and Rylee with the note, merger coming soon.

What did that mean?

She worried her bottom lip as she peered at the picture closely. Both of them were sitting across from each other around a conference table grinning like Cheshire cats.

So much for thinking that Pete was at home, pining over her. Giselle closed the phone and inhaled, So much for thinking that she should confess to him that she had been lying.

He was an eighteen-year-old boy. He had lots of life to live, and so did she.

****

"You are seven weeks pregnant?" Anthea said softly. She was a middle-aged woman with an excellent bedside manner. She managed to make her patients feel as if they were her only priority. One time a long time ago, Giselle would fantasize that Anthea was her mother.

She was the reason she had even thought of doing medicine.

Giselle looked at her now to gauge whether she was disapproving of her, but she only saw interest.

"I take it this was not planned," Anthea said and then patted her hand.

"No." Giselle shook her head. "It wasn't. I need to take some time off and assess what I am going to do next."

Anthea wrote up the sick leave slip with a flourish and then looked up at her. "Since you are here, let's do the whole works, the confirmation, the checkup, and everything to make sure the little one is progressing as she should."

"She?" Giselle raised her eyebrows.

Anthea chuckled. "I love using she as my universal gender language."

"Okay, then." Giselle sighed.

An hour later she was sent on her way with a whole stack of literature on what to expect next, an admonition to train lightly for the next couple of months if she wanted to train at all and to keep her stress levels to a minimum.

She was just about to open her car door when she heard her name.

She groaned and looked around. It was Sheryl Wiley. She was dressed in a deep burgundy suit, with lipstick to match. She looked like what she was, a high-powered executive.

"Hey," Giselle said, trying to keep her voice from sounding absolutely defeated. "How are you?"

"I am good." Sheryl walked over to her. She glanced at the literature in her hands and then raised an eyebrow. "How are you?"

"Good. Great," Giselle said tiredly. "I have to go."

Sheryl squinted at her. "So you are having the baby then? I was hoping you would."

Giselle inhaled raggedly. So Pete had told Sheryl. Blabbermouth Pete. He just couldn't leave things alone.

"Pete hasn't said a word of any of this to me, Sheryl said. "Preston did. I have been debating reaching out to you about this, but I have a feeling that you wanted space."

"I did." Giselle sighed. "And I still haven't decided. Didn't Pete tell you this is not his child?"

Sheryl frowned at her and then stepped back. "Oh Giselle, there is no need to be so hostile or push me away, I have stayed out of this, remember. We are all respecting your space. If you ever need help, anytime at all, call me. I am here."

Giselle nodded. "Thanks, er, I have to go."

She went into the car and had to blink several times before she could see to put the keys into the ignition switch to start the car.

****

She took her time to drive back to the track club. She headed to Kurt's office. He was on the phone when she entered. He looked over the sick leave and approved it.

"Have a seat, Giselle."

She sat down across from him, "I don't want a lecture."

"I heard from coach Stevens. It would have been nice if you could have told me that you weren't planning to renew your contract at the end of the year."

"I can't talk about any of that now. I am waiting on his university to respond. I don't want to jinx it."

Kurt looked at her still flat belly pointedly. "So you are keeping the baby then?"

"I don't know!". She really didn't know; the question was becoming tiring.

"Have you told Pete the truth?" Kurt leaned forward; a lock of his curly hair hung on his brow.

"We are no longer speaking to each other." Giselle gritted out. "It's over."

"I was thinking," Kurt inhaled, "we could get married. You have the baby. I train you exclusively for the next five years. After that, we can go our separate ways."

Giselle had been fiddling with her phone, her head snapped up so fast she knew she had given herself mild whiplash.

"Say what now?"

"You heard." Kurt drummed his fingers on the desk. "It could be an option. Your child would be legitimate."

"Nobody cares about that in the twenty-first century." Giselle shook her head slightly. "I am hallucinating, aren't I? I swear you just asked me to marry you."

"Think about it," Kurt said, "I think we could make a go of this personally and professionally. I still have feelings for you. I haven't managed to dismiss them as thoroughly as you have. Do med school here, I'll finance it."

"I was thinking of switching to Physiotherapy." Giselle was still trying to wrap her head around the proposal.

"We have accredited Physio programs at the university across the road," Kurt said, "or are you afraid of going to the same school as Pete."

"I can't think about any of this right now." Giselle got up. "I am waiting to hear from Coach Stevens' university. When I do, I'll know what my next moves will be."

"But promise me you'll think about what I said." Kurt smiled. "When you decide, I am here."

As if on cue her phone pinged, she waited until she entered the car before she checked the message. It was from Groover University.

We are pleased to inform you…

"Yes!" She read through the note.

And then she looked for the scholarship offer. Based on your grades and your athletic standing…we are offering a grant…

A grant, a small grant. So minute she couldn't take it seriously.

Giselle closed her eyes. A grant was not a scholarship.

She already had two scholarship offers, and she had two more weeks to formally accept. She had to choose now. She looked at the brochures that Dr. Athena had given her. They all had happy pregnant ladies on the front.

Her heart beat in despair. She was not a happy pregnant lady; she had never felt so overwhelmed in her life.

"God, I need help, and I need it now," she whispered. "I need to know what to do."

She waited expectantly for God to answer her, but no answer came.

Chapter Thirteen

She was in the middle of eating lunch when the security guard rang her phone.

"Sharla Phipps is out here to see you." The security guard said.

Aunt Sharla!

"Send her in," Giselle said quickly. She had no idea that Sharla was in Jamaica. Her aunt usually told them when she was coming.

She opened the door and watched as Sharla parked the car. It was Jordan's car, so he knew that Sharla was here. Maybe Tiana and Elsa knew too. Why was she left in the dark?

Sharla exited the car and gave her a happy smile.

Giselle's heart melted. Sharla was the closest thing to a mother that she had through the years. She was present for all the majors. She made an effort to be close to all of them, her orphaned nieces and nephews, even Saint, Walter and Preston. Nine children plus she had two of her own. And she managed to be a cool and strict aunt at the same time.

Sharla was a pretty Indian woman who look as if she was on the slow road to aging. She wore her hair in a lopsided lob. She had taken to dye her greys a vivid shade of red, so she had red streaks all through her hair.

"They are coming to get you," Sharla would laugh at them. The women in our family grey prematurely.

Her aunt was in her mid-forties, a mother of two with a thriving career and a husband who loved her to pieces.

"I didn't know you were in Jamaica," Giselle said brightly.

"It is a quick stop; I am leaving tomorrow." Sharla looked at her intently. "Tiana called and told me you were in a crisis. I have accumulated quite a few free miles. So here I am, Superwoman coming to rescue her niece."

"I love you." Giselle threw herself on Sharla.

"I love you more," Sharla murmured. "My baby girl. I still can't think of you as an adult."

"Tiana was wrong though I am not in a crisis. I just needed some time to get my priorities straight."

She moved out of her aunt's arms and headed for the couch. "Would you like something to drink? I think I have water."

"Just water?" Sharla looked at her half-empty plate. "At least you are eating. That looks yum."

Giselle nodded. "It was yum. I am full now."

Sharla sat across from her putting her tote bag beside her and looked around, "I love this apartment, nice and airy and chic. The décor screams Giselle."

"Thanks." Giselle hugged a cushion to her middle. "Pete and Shawn did it while I was in Europe in the summer. Jordan shaved off a couple of millions when they were selling it to me."

"Peter Wiley." Sharla raised an eyebrow. "Couldn't you go farther afield to find yourself a boyfriend, Gis?"

"He's not…" Giselle bit her lip; the denial was going to be a lie. Pete was her boyfriend. Had been her boyfriend.

Sharla looked at her knowingly. "What's with the women in our family and the Wiley men?"

Giselle rested her head back on the settee. She was not going to accept or deny anything.

"How is Jordan taking this? Or Guy? Or Case?"

"They don't know yet." Giselle sighed. "I was considering… er…"

"Having an abortion," Sharla said wearily. "I heard."

"What? Why does Tiana talk so much?" Giselle grumbled.

"Once, a long time ago, I made a silly mistake," Sharla murmured, "I was fifteen and stupid. Your mother Monique was my guardian, as you know, and she was strict because of that. I was a little bit more sheltered than the typical teenager my age."

"Anyway, that was not an excuse. I had the biggest crush on this boy in a higher grade in high school. His name was Leroy. He was charming, or what I thought was charming, he was good looking in a rugged country boy sort of way. He was going places too, everybody said so."

Giselle chuckled.

"And then we sort of started seeing each other. Monique was against me having any sort of relationship. I thought she was crazy; how could she understand the love I had for Leroy. At the time she was single, and she dedicated her life to raising Hannah and me when our mother left us. She didn't have a life. By simple logic, I just assumed she had no idea what she was talking about when she warned me about Leroy. The stupidity of youth."

Giselle nodded she had heard that story about Monique a million times before. What she hadn't known was that Sharla had a relationship before Tanner.

"It wasn't a relationship," Sharla said as if reading her mind. "It was a three-minute sex romp at the back of the classroom while there was a concert at school. To my shame, he didn't even coax me to go with him. I went of my own free will."

Sharla clasped her hands together and then looked down at them. "When I found out that I was pregnant, I didn't think about it, I didn't tell a soul, I knew of a doctor who did abortions. It was whispered about that he did it and I just went and got it done. It cost me all the money that I had saved up, but I did it. I never told Leroy, or Monique or Hannah, nobody knew."

"Are you saying I should do the same?" Giselle asked slowly.

"I told you my deepest darkest secret because I don't want you to repeat my mistake," Sharla looked at her. "There isn't one day that goes by that I have not regretted it. It has a tendency to sit with you, the knowledge that you did this thing. In my case, it was the shame of it, the disapproval of my sister. In your case, it would be sheer convenience, because having a baby doesn't fit into your life right now."

Giselle nodded. "I hear you."

"Besides, if you really wanted to do it, you would have done it already. You told your sisters and Pete and your coach, everybody. You don't want to do it."

Giselle wriggled her toes. "I have been thinking about it, weighing all my options. I ask myself the question what would my mother do? What would the saintly Monique Kennedy Pryce do?"

"She would be horrified that you even thought of abortion." Sharla mused. "She would tell you not to. I never told her about mine, even as an adult. I was afraid to because I never wanted her to be ashamed of me. In Monique's eyes, there would be no justification for it, not even rape. If you don't want the child, give it up for adoption."

"And my career? All the things I have worked for?" Giselle asked.

"Ah Gis, that's a flimsy reason to do it. You are an adult you have your own apartment; you make money, you have a degree. You are surrounded by support."

"But I don't want to be a mother," Giselle said plaintively. "It's not a burning desire of mine. I know I sound like a bad person, but I just don't want to be a mother. At least not now. I haven't had some miraculous change in my personality where I am suddenly motherly inclined. It wasn't a part of my plans. I just don't want this."

"How does Pete feel about this?" Sharla asked.

"He doesn't want me to have an abortion." Giselle shrugged. "I don't think he has thought past that. He has no clue that his life is about to be upended if I have this child."

Sharla ran her fingers through her hair, pulling it off her face. "I know it has to be tough. He is still a teenager. Having a child is a huge responsibility, even for adults who are in a committed relationship."

"Tell you what, have the baby, and we'll adopt him."

"Him?" Giselle raised her eyebrows.

"I have no preference girl or boy. Even though I would love to have a little girl. I was talking to Tanner about it, we'd be happy to take the child."

"You all have been discussing me, have you?"

"Yes," Sharla said solemnly, "you can't just close yourself off and not expect your family to be concerned."

"I don't know about this, Aunt Sharla," Giselle frowned. "In all of this, I never thought of adoption."

"Well, that option is now on the table," Sharla said, "discuss it with Pete. It will free you both to move on with your lives."

"I'll talk to him." Giselle squeezed the cushion even closer to her. "I guess you'll be the first to know, I applied to the university where my old coach works and got through, but I was offered a grant. They don't give scholarships to pregnant athletes."

"Oh honey," Sharla said, "I wish I could pay for it for you, but we have our two in university too. It would be perfect if you came up, we live quite close to Groover University."

"I know." Giselle nodded.

"What about Toddy, can't he fund this?" Sharla said, "You could come and stay with us until you have the baby."

Giselle shook her head. "No, I can't ask Toddy. He just gave up his business and sold the house. I don't know what kind of financial footing he is standing on right now."

"You could ask your cousins?" Sharla murmured. "Jordan, Guy or Case…"

"No. Never," Giselle said fiercely. "I'll work out something. I'll let you know what I decide."

"Patch things up with Pete and tell him the truth. It does nobody any good to have this lie about him not being the child's father hanging out there. You rob him when you do that, Gis."

Giselle inhaled. "I know."

"Do the right thing," Sharla said, "and do it before it is too late."

****

She paced the apartment after Sharla left. It had been good talking through things with her aunt. Sharla had gotten her to put things into perspective. She was having the baby she had to let Toddy know.

She took a deep breath and called Toddy.

"Hey Toddy," she said nervously. She didn't know why she was nervous; she was an adult. Toddy was no longer her guardian.

"Giselle!" Toddy said jovially, "I was just watching your Diamond League videos with some colleagues of mine, remember that race where you came from behind and left the field in your dust?"

"Yes," Giselle said quickly, knowing Toddy he was gearing up for a long conversation extolling her virtues.

"Er… Toddy…there is something that I must tell you."

"What is it?" Toddy sobered up, responding to the seriousness in her voice.

"I am pregnant." Giselle cleared her throat. "It was officially confirmed by a doctor today."

"Oookay," Toddy said. "This is unexpected."

"I know." Giselle inhaled raggedly. "I know."

"Who is the guy, I didn't know you were in a relationship."

"I er had a thing. Well…" Giselle cleared her throat. "I've been with Pete since my birthday this year."

"Pete, as in Peter Wiley?" Toddy sounded alarmed.

"Yes." Gisele hissed. "Peter Wiley."

"Good genes, good family," Toddy said, "I thought you were laser focused. I wouldn't have pegged you to be the first one to become a mother. Motherhood changes things, you know."

"I heard being a parent is the hardest job in the world," Giselle murmured.

"And also the most rewarding." Toddy forced some joviality in his voice. "Well, if you need anything at all, you know I am here for you."

"Thanks, Toddy."

"Is it terribly traditional of me that I am thinking of

marriage?" Toddy mused. "I mean, I can have a meeting with Preston mano o mano, and we discuss the wedding and all of that, trash out the details."

Giselle chuckled. "You'll do no such thing. We are living in the twenty-first century. I'll marry Pete only when I am sure that it's the right time for us. I don't want to tie him up further than I have already done. Besides, Sharla and Tanner want to adopt the child."

"What?" Toddy asked. "And Pete's family is okay with this? Preston Wiley is okay with you, giving away his grandchild to Sharla?"

"I haven't told them yet," Giselle mumbled.

"This will be war." Toddy groaned. "You sure you want to do this, Gis?"

"I am not sure of anything." Giselle exhaled raggedly. "I just know that I am not ready to be a mother."

"Okay, ma'am," Toddy said, disappointed. "Anything at all you need, you ask me, okay."

"I am good for now, Toddy." Giselle's voice cracked. "I was thinking of going to stay with Sharla, I applied to another university in Florida. We'll talk later."

When she hung up the phone, she texted Pete. I have decided, meet me at your house at 6.

She was really going to do this. She was having a baby.

She looked at herself in the mirror; she didn't look different. She certainly felt different on the inside, but she didn't look it.

Chapter Fourteen

Pete got the text from Giselle when he was in the middle of his Advanced Calculus class. His heart lurched. What had she decided to do?

He didn't hear much of what his instructor was droning on and on about after that. He found advanced calculus pretty easy anyway.

Giselle had decided and it worried him as to what that meant.

"Hey Pete," Rylee tapped him on the shoulder. She was sitting behind him. "Are we still meeting after class. I have this app idea that will blow your mind, and maybe our bank account."

Pete looked back at her blankly. "Yes, of course. We are meeting at Wiley Complex conference room. I have a thing at six, though. So I might take a raincheck on the new app idea."

Rylee raised an eyebrow, "Queen Giselle is now called a

thing?"

Pete grinned. "Stop fishing."

Rylee twirled her hair around her fingers and affected a sultry pose. "Oh, Pete dahling, we hate each other because we both want you."

Pete shook his head and turned back around to meet the lecturer's stern stare.

"Mr. Wiley," Professor Linton smirked, "could you come up here and solve question two. The rest of the class would appreciate your input."

He was trying to embarrass him. Pete grinned and got up. "With pleasure."

He ended up teaching the rest of the class, he explained the concepts much better than the Professor did anyway.

Professor Linton did not look perturbed by it.

After class, he went to the Wiley Complex, conference room one. His father and Walter and the Wiley's official lawyer, Bryan Blair were there.

Rylee was behind him with her father and their lawyer. It was overkill, but ever since he floated the idea to his father that he wanted to start an app business with Rylee and they had gotten the multimillion-dollar contract with the bank, the writing was on the wall to make everything official and legally sound.

At Walter's insistence, Pete had started a limited liability company for his gaming apps development business when he was just sixteen. Rylee had done the same when she started to develop her apps too. This was somewhat of a merger.

"Hello Mr. Wiley," Preston grinned at him with a proud twinkle in his eye.

"Hello Mr. Wileys," he greeted both his uncle and dad when he walked into the room. "And Mr. Blair."

The lawyer nodded at him.

It was a pretty straightforward meeting all of it was outlined in legal documents. Wiley Apps was made a subsidiary of Wiley Inc.

They even had a new address, upstairs Case's building. They had a whole suite of offices for themselves. And they had the support of Wiley Inc. with key staff.

He had the majority shares in the company, forty percent, Rylee had twenty and Wiley Inc had the rest. Rylee could not sell her shares to anyone but the Wiley's.

Her father blustered a little at that but soon calmed down when his lawyer whispered in his ear.

It was a done deal by five o'clock. He was the majority shareholder of his own business.

He looked at his watch. He needed to check out his new office space and beat rush hour traffic to get to Giselle's house by six.

His father and uncles had other plans, though. One by one, his other uncles showed up. Even Case was there. His new landlord.

"We have a brief shareholders meeting," Preston said solemnly.

"Okay," Pete nodded, "well carry on then."

"Wait!" Jordan said, "didn't your lawyer tell you that you are now officially a shareholder? You own a Wiley business. That Wiley Inc investment is your share of the parent company. You now have voting rights."

"Oh," Pete widened his eyes. "I had no clue."

"Welcome to the conglomerate." Guy chuckled. "By the way, be warned, Walter has us in intense competition when he ranks our companies' performances."

Pete chuckled. "Well okay then. I'll endeavor not to come last in the rankings."

"He reminds me of a young Preston. You look just like

Preston at eighteen, looking at you is like going back in time," Walter said huskily. "Remember the first time you came up to this floor? You were all wide-eyed and scared of the Big Boss?"

"Yes." Pete nodded. "I remember. Are you guys going to be all sentimental, and we have a group hug and sing kumbaya around the conference table?"

Jordan laughed. "No. We are meeting because we have to vote on the townhouse project."

"We have acquired the land beside us, the one with the dated house. It sits on two acres of land. I already submitted the plans to the parish council. I need the permission of this board to go ahead and start the project."

"Will it be similar to the Wiley complex?" Pete asked, interestedly.

"Yes." Jordan nodded. "Very similar. It is more property, though, a bigger complex. You can take a walk to my office and see the layout."

"Mmm." Pete nodded. "I might want to buy one for investment purposes."

His uncles laughed.

Preston was the first to sober up. "It's a Wiley Project. Technically they are all yours. You are a shareholder now."

"Cool." Pete glanced at his watch, "I have to go, I have a meeting with Gis."

Six pairs of eyes looked at him interestedly.

"We don't want to get involved in your situation with Giselle," Jordan said, "Preston told us to back off, and we are listening. Just know that we are here whenever you want to talk."

"How do you know there is a situation with Giselle and me?" Pete asked suspiciously.

"Giselle is our cousin, Jordan said. "Sharla is here to

support her for something so mysterious she can't say a word. We know something is going on, we are not blind."

"We also know that Giselle is independent and stubborn," Case said. "What is she up to? What's wrong?"

Pete looked at his father and then at his uncles. "I can't tell you."

"She is pregnant," Saint said, "and she is contemplating where to go from here as in whether to keep the baby or not."

"Say what?" His uncles started talking over each other. Pete backed out of the room. He should have known that Saint would know, he was a private investigator after all.

He waved to his father, who was standing a little bit from the fray.

Preston waved back.

Pete reached the bank of elevators and breathed a sigh of relief. Things became a little convoluted when you had a large family.

His relief was cut short when the elevator door opened to reveal his mother standing there.

"Going down?" She smiled at him brightly.

Pete groaned. His mother knew about Giselle's pregnancy, and she had not said a thing to him about it for the past two weeks. She was waiting for him to tell her.

Her restraint was phenomenal. He stepped into the elevator with her. He was taller than her by a few inches, and she was tall.

"Hello, Mom." She smelled good and looked good. Sometimes he marveled at the idea that the modelesque Sheryl Wiley was his mother.

She didn't look like she had a son his age. And now she would be a grandmother if Giselle had the baby. He longed to ask her how she felt about the situation, but he held back. He didn't know for sure what Giselle's decision would be.

"How did it go?" Sheryl asked. "Your meeting?"

"It went well. I am the majority shareholder in Wiley Apps. Case is going to be my landlord. So no more working from my room. I have a suite of offices above his studio beside the advertising agency."

"I am proud of you, hun." Sheryl reached up to kiss him.

"Thank you." The elevator stopped, and they stepped out together. A few people stopped and did a double take. They did that every time he entered the Wiley building because of the resemblance to their boss.

"So where are you off to?" Sheryl asked when they exited the lobby.

"Giselle's." He inhaled. "Mom…"

"Yes." Sheryl stopped and stood in front of him.

"I know you know."

"What do I know?" Sheryl asked him solemnly. She wasn't making it easy for him.

"Giselle is pregnant with my baby."

Sheryl hugged him to her. It was spontaneous.

Then she pulled away from him and inhaled, tears were in her eyes. "Fourteen days, five hours and twenty minutes, that's how long it took you to tell me."

"Giselle just texted me to tell me that she decided what she is going to do. I didn't want to talk about it before I hear what she is going to do."

Sheryl nodded. "I know. We'll talk when you get in later. Maybe we can have a family meeting then."

"Yes." Pete nodded.

"You'll be fine." Sheryl pinched him on his cheek. "Love you."

"Love you too, mom," Pete said bemusedly.

****

Pete drove toward Giselle's apartment. He had stopped speculating about what she had decided and instead spent most of his time trying to psychoanalyze himself.

What was it about Giselle that had him so fascinated? He could never quite work it out.

Yes, she was pretty but so were most of the girls around him. As a matter of fact, he didn't need to go far to find two other variations of Giselle.

Giselle and Elsa could be twins, their eye colors were different, and they had different hairstyles, but that was all. Tiana had a different coloring, but she looked like a different version of Giselle too. And he had zero romantic feelings toward Tiana and Elsa.

As a matter of fact, Elsa was the first one of the triplets he had met. She was at Guy's farm when he had seen her first. And he had not been the least bit bothered.

But then he had met Giselle, and it was as if all the chemicals in his body was triggered. One look was all it took. He remembered it clearly, he was twelve years old. His poor heart had taken off on a gallop. He had felt breathless, butterflies in his belly, and shaking hands.

He had told his father about it that very day, and Preston had laughed. It's a crush you'll get over it.

When Giselle had dramatically told him to butt out of her life, he had taken it hard and had to be ignominiously taken to a psychiatrist because he couldn't stop crying. He had never been as depressed. It was as if his whole world had plummeted.

Dr. Levy had actually prescribed medication for his chemical imbalance as she had called it.

His mother and father had argued over him taking the medication. They had even thought of him changing schools to avoid Giselle.

In the end, he had to take the pills, especially when Dr. Levy said the chemicals could cause havoc in his brain for up to two years. "If he still has it, then we are going into the territory of limerence," Dr. Levy had said sternly.

He had to attend a few weeks of therapy to learn to cope with his feelings for Gis. The doctor had declared him better after his feelings for Giselle had mellowed into something controllable. Dr. Levy had told his parents that she had never seen a case as bad as his.

He remembered her explaining to him what was happening to his brain, was like a temporary mental illness.

All of that had normalized through the years, and then this year, he slept with Giselle. He shouldn't have.

It had created a deep bond between them.

And now she was going to have his baby or not…

****

Pete got out of the car when he reached the apartment. He rang the doorbell instead of using his key.

Giselle opened the door. She was in a red t-shirt that hit her mid-thigh. Her hair was in two fat plats, she didn't look older than sixteen. His heart did its familiar lurch when he saw her.

"Hey, you," he said huskily, "here I am."

"Hey," She stepped back from the door.

Pete went in and closed the door and leaned on it.

"Gis…"

"Pete…"

"Yes," Pete said, hoping his voice was encouraging. Giselle held all the cards. It was her show. He was at her mercy.

"I er, I am sorry about the last couple of weeks. I lied to you when I told you that I slept with Kurt."

Pete folded his arms and looked at her. "You shouldn't plant doubt in a man's mind, Gis."

"I know. I just thought," Giselle swallowed, "I thought it would be easier without you around guilt tripping me. Anyway, I am having the baby."

She grimaced. "I can't do an abortion even though it was my first panicked thought. I am sorry for deliberating it so long. I know it was driving you crazy."

"Thank you." Pete exhaled raggedly.

"I read an article yesterday," Giselle sighed. "It was entitled ten reasons why you should not become a mother. All the reasons on it sounded as if it were talking about me. I need to work on my patience. I am not ready to put somebody before my career. I am feeling pressured about this; I travel a lot for my job. I am making a million and one excuses. I am just not ready."

Pete's voice cracked. "Okay."

"Sharla came by today, and we discussed her adopting the baby. Before you protest, there are some advantages to this, I'll be in Florida when I have the baby. I might do university there. I'll tell you more about that later."

Pete watched her without saying anything. He hadn't quite recovered from the line I am going to have the baby, and now he was hearing that she wanted to give it up for adoption.

"Can you think about a better parent than Sharla? She has always been there for all of us."

Pete still hadn't moved a muscle.

"You'll have your freedom, and so will I. I am not ready to be a mother. And we can get to see our child. We'll know where our baby is and when the baby grows up, he or she will know who we are. Say something Pete!"

"No." Pete shook his head. "I was given up for adoption when I was a baby. I don't want that for my child."

"So, what are you proposing?" Giselle whispered.

"I'll take care of my child, thank you," Pete said dryly. "I am not trying to make you feel bad or anything, but I think I can cope just fine. I didn't expect fatherhood at my age, but I can roll with the punches. My father and my uncles took care of themselves when they were much younger than I was, and they ended up quite fine."

Giselle hung her head. "I am terrible, aren't I?"

"No," Pete sighed, "you are not terrible. I think you are making the right choice about having the baby."

"Well, at least that's something," Giselle sighed. "My life is now in flux."

"Not necessarily," Pete sighed, "I didn't want to suggest this before, I wanted you to make up your mind about this without undue influence. I talked to my dad about it."

"Your dad again," Giselle muttered under her breath.

Pete chuckled dryly. "I'll pay all your expenses for whatever school you want to go to. In exchange, I get to keep my child."

Giselle sat down in the settee hard. "So, Kurt Yu offered marriage and a chance to be my trainer for five years, aunt Sharla offered adoption, and Pete Wiley offers me an all-expense paid education, all I'll need to do is hand over my baby to him, and here I was thinking I had limited options."

"Kurt Yu offered you marriage?" Pete narrowed his eyes at her. "Really? Does he think this is his child?"

"He doesn't think that because I never had sex with him." Giselle snorted. "He was just trying to hitch his cart to mine. Kurt has always had this bright idea that I am his golden goose. His gateway to opening his own training center and attracting top athletes. That's why I even brought him up as a potential father. I thought he would be the first one to encourage me to have the abortion, but he surprised me."

"Your reasoning was warped." Pete rubbed the back of his neck. "That may be the case, but he had always had feelings for you. I guess I should be happy that you didn't say yes. You'll always be in high demand. I should be happy that we broke up. I don't have to spend my time being jealous when you inevitably leave."

"I need to think about this." Giselle grimaced. "I don't know if I can take your money."

"You'll take it," Pete said dispassionately, "you are a pragmatist. You have your dreams; you need someone to finance them. I can finance them, and I want my child."

"That's unfair." Giselle glared at him. "You make me sound so cold and uncaring. I have worked hard all my life. I have been focused and conscientious, and I…"

Tears gathered in Giselle's eyes. "I shouldn't have gotten involved with you."

Pete pushed himself from the door and went to stand in front of her. He touched her cheek softly. "Maybe you are right. I am sorry about everything."

"Me too." Giselle swallowed, "we break up so many times."

"Maybe we weren't meant to be," Pete whispered. "Not every story is a love story."

Giselle nodded jerkily. "I'll update you on the baby and then when the baby is born you can come and take her... him…"

Pete reached down and kissed her hard on the lips.

She clutched the front of his shirt. Pulling him even closer to her.

It was a heartfelt, passionate kiss that went on forever. Pete stepped away from her. He had to put a stop to it, or they would just end up upstairs, and then he would be a little bit more ensnared. He had to think of his sanity.

"If we are going to make a clean break. I think now is a good time to start." He backed away from her. "Keep me updated about the baby."

He left the house with his heart hammering against his chest. Even with a few gulps of air the pain in his chest didn't loosen up much. He was going to be a single father, and he had just lost the woman that he loved.

Chapter Fifteen

We laugh until we had to cry, And we loved right down to our last goodbye

We were the best, I think we'll ever be, Just you and me... for just a moment.

Rylee was humming that song when Pete stepped into their newly furnished conference room four weeks later. You could still smell the new scents wafting from the furniture. The place had an open area with eight cubicles, three private offices, a large conference room and a kitchen.

It was too large for them now, but they needed help with the bank app, and they had his various game apps to develop.

Time goes on, people touch and then they are gone...

The song hit him to the core. Today was the day when Giselle left Jamaica. It had him feeling raw.

"Turn it off." He growled at Rylee.

"Somebody is in a bad mood." Rylee frowned, "what's eating you?"

"Giselle is leaving today, and I just had a morning exam. Can't remember what I wrote. Today sucks."

Rylee made a face. "That's tough. Are you sure that you are going to be able to concentrate on the task at hand? HR lined up a bunch of interviews for us today.

"Yeah, sure." Pete sat down across from Rylee. "I am mature enough to handle business and school."

"And fatherhood soon." Rylee looked at him, skeptically, "are you sure that you'll be able to do all of those?"

"Yes," Pete said bitingly. He had been getting that question a lot lately.

His family didn't think he could. They were constantly bugging him about it especially because Giselle was giving birth sometime in mid-May and she was sending the baby out with Sharla not long after.

At least he would have a place to stay by then. Jordan's team had stepped up construction on his apartment. And all his aunts and his mom had volunteered to furnish the nursery.

One thing was for sure, he was not going to be short of any baby related paraphernalia, nor was he going to be short of experience in how to handle a newborn.

Shawn had recently given birth to a son they decided to name Cairo. He was a sweet little thing who so far looked a lot like Case.

"You never know what you are going to get in the gene pool," Shawn said proudly when she looked down at her son. "He is absolutely sweet, isn't he?"

"He is." Pete nodded. "I never thought of newborns as adorable before. Petra looked a little like she was crushed up."

Shawn laughed. "Your kid will probably look just like Jordan because of the genetic combination but then again who knows, he might look like Sheryl's side of the family."

He had slept at Jordan's house for a week because Shawn insisted that he needed to learn about newborns. She had him changing diapers and doing all sorts of new parent things.

"How is the practice coming?" Jordan whispered when he found Pete cuddling the semi-sleeping baby in the kitchen.

"Okay," Pete whispered back. "It is not as hard as I hear all the mother's warning me about.

"Because he is a newborn." Jordan took his baby from Pete. "They are good at this stage. There is a reason why they have a term the terrible twos."

"I'll manage." Pete tucked the blanket around Cairo and stepped back.

"We'll be here." Jordan had nodded. "I need to go over the changes you requested for your patio area."

"Pete!" Rylee snapped her fingers in front of his face.

"Yes," Pete jolted back to the present, he had to get his head in the game. Giselle was leaving at the right time when he would be too busy to hurt or miss her much.

****

Pregnancy and school were not comfortable bedfellows. Giselle was thrown into the deep end as soon as she stepped on the university campus, which would be her home for the next three years. She would commute from Sharla's house, which was just twenty minutes away, she had the use of Sharla's car.

Coach Stevens didn't sign her up immediately for the track and field program, she had to see the campus counselor every week.

"Part of our policy," he had told her when she protested. "I want your head back in the game in a couple of months. I don't want you to quit after you have the baby. The statistics are not in your favor, most women take some time off after having a baby, and that's fair. You are going to need nerves of steel to stay focused even with your plan to hand the baby over to your boyfriend. You will be a mass of hormones and emotions. You know track and field is a good percentage mental as well as physical. I want you prepared."

He was right.

She read up the literature for her program and felt instantly intimidated. What had she let herself in for? The MSc Physiotherapy is a demanding program of core modules; all of which must be completed successfully to pass.

For the love of all that was holy. Giselle sat down and cradled her stomach after walking out of the admin offices.

She had been introduced to her faculty advisor and was shown the brutal realities of motherhood, studying, and doing athletics.

"Just remember you are not superwoman." Her advisor Judy, a mother of four, had said to her with a smile. "Are you sure you are up for this?"

No, I am not, Giselle had screamed in her head. What on earth was she thinking?

First of all, for the past two weeks, while she was in America, she missed Pete to the point where it was like an ache.

Obviously, he wasn't missing her as much, he had his new business to get off the ground and his new semester. His texts to her had been terse and sparsely worded.

She also missed her sisters and her apartment and Toddy and Myrna and even Kurt and her track club mates. Everything here was new, and the adjustment was hard.

And she was pregnant.

Maybe an abortion was not a bad idea, after all. She was five months along and barely showing. She could always say she miscarried. She got up from the bench that she had sat on in her despair and looked around, it was a pretty campus. She hadn't really taken in the aesthetics of the place yet.

The Physiotherapy faculty had their own building, a tree with yellow blooms flanked the front. It was starkly pretty in the overcast January day.

She was going to do it. This felt like déjà vu, but it was the only way out. This time she wasn't panicked. This time she was just overwhelmed and staring in the hard, cold face of reality.

She looked up a board-certified place on Google, and she was heading for the parking lot to her car.

This time she wasn't going to turn on her radio. This time she wasn't going to let her conscience override her. She needed to do this. Only God could stop her now. If he really didn't want her to do this, he would stop her. God doesn't give us more than we can bear. She heard Myrna's voice in her head, and you can't bear this Giselle. This, all of this, is too much.

If God didn't want her to go through with this, he would have to give her a sure and true sign. He would have to stop her dead in her tracks. Tell her straight from heaven. Slow her down. Stop her, but she was going through with this.

She realized that she was feverishly rambling in her head and slowed down a bit. Taking a deep gulp of cool air. She was almost knocked sideways by a group of girls who were heading toward the physiotherapy building.

"Excuse me," they said almost in chorus, they flashed her a smile.

She counted four of them as they walked by. One was blond with blue eyes, the other three were racially ambiguous.

"No problem," She said under her breath.

One of them glanced back at her, she had a light tan, long

brown hair, and green eyes. She stopped. "That's a Jamaican accent!"

Giselle nodded. "Yes, it is."

"I am Jamaican too." She squealed. "Well, I mean, my mother is Jamaican. I vacation there every summer. My name is Danica, everybody calls me Dani."

Giselle smiled. "I am Giselle."

Dani's friends had left her behind, and she didn't care. She was obviously excited about talking to Giselle.

"Giselle is such a pretty name." Dani laughed, "I had to stop for two reasons, one you are Jamaican and two, you look a lot, and I mean a lot like my mom. You have the same complexion and facial structure."

"I do?" Giselle raised an eyebrow skeptically.

"I am mixed race. Can't you see the melanin?" Dani held out her hand and giggled. "I get a deep tan in the summer, trust me."

Giselle glanced furtively at her watch. She didn't have the time to be standing around and talking about tanning.

"I have to go." She smiled at Dani politely.

"No," Dani widened her eyes, "I can't lose you now, Giselle. I have to find out why you look like my mom."

Was the girl serious? Giselle grimaced. Was she one of those that thought that all people of color looked alike?

"Wait, let me show you," Danica pulled her phone from her purse. She scrolled through her photos and handed it to Giselle with a flourish, "tada…"

There was a picture of Hannah Kennedy and a white man hugging each other before a church.

Giselle gasped. She looked so much like her dead aunt and her mother and to a lesser extent Sharla.

"Told you," Dani said smugly. "That's my mom and dad."

"What's her name?" Giselle glanced up from the phone.

"My mom's name is Sara Hunt. Well, it was Craig before Hunt."

Giselle blinked her eyes rapidly. "Craig? Doesn't ring a bell. I don't know if we are related to any Craig's. Well, I had a teacher once in high school named Craig, but we weren't related…"

"Mmm, we shall see." Dani grinned. "What's your surname?"

"Pryce." Giselle cleared her throat. "My mother's maiden name was Kennedy."

She handed Dani back her phone. "This is intriguing."

"I'd say." Dani grinned. "I'd love to have a cousin. I am an only child of only children."

"Cousins plural," Giselle said. "I am one of three."

"As in triplets?" Dani squealed.

"Yes," Giselle smiled despite herself. Dani's excitement was infectious. "I have other cousins too."

"We must get to the bottom of this then," Dani said excitedly. "This must be the reason why I came to this part of the campus today. I usually don't come this way, but the Christian Fellowship Group decided that they were going to take a club picture in front of the Physio building. We do one every year for the website. Last year it was before the lake over at SoSci, but this year we are here because of the tree. It is pretty, isn't it?"

Giselle nodded.

"They needed to plant more of these on campus." Dani grinned. "But I think it is fortuitous meeting you like this. I wasn't going to come; I have an Ethics class debate in two hours, and I am not very prepared."

"Well then…" Giselle smiled, "I won't hold you up."

"It's not a hold-up, this is a blessing!" Dani grinned. "I'll wing the debate; I am a natural at debating. The topic is

Abortion, we are looking at the moral, legal, and religious views. I memorized some of the raw data. I kinda have a photographic memory. Oh goodness, did I leave that paper," she started rummaging in her bag, a panicked look on her face.

"I have it," Dani sighed in relief. "I thought I left my facts; see I have this: Do Fetuses Cry Paper. I am going to put it up on the projector and sway the audience with the sight of the fetus. Of course, there is the famous video too, but I don't have time for it, and it is a little disturbing."

Giselle felt a weird feeling wash over her as Dani continued to talk.

"Do they cry?" She asked Dani hoarsely.

"Oh, yes, they do! Research shows that fetuses may learn to express their displeasure by crying silently while still in the womb as early as in the 20th week of pregnancy."

"I er..." Giselle blinked rapidly. "Really?"

"At twenty weeks they are the size of a sweet potato," Dani showed her the size, "and they still have space to twist and turn in the uterus." Dani laughed oblivious that her babbling was like a slap of cold water to the face.

"Oh my goodness, I just met you, and here I am jabbering. I am the first speaker for my group."

As if on cue, Giselle's baby kicked her for the first time as if to say, is this enough of a miracle for you, Giselle Pryce? Or do I have to send you another sign that you shouldn't go through with this?

Dani told her a chirpy goodbye, and Giselle slowly walked to her car. She was twenty weeks pregnant. What are the odds that just when she was short-circuiting, a girl she had never before seen in her life appeared out of nowhere and told her stuff about babies and abortion?

She had gotten her answer. She would not think about that

ever again. She would have to cope.

Maybe she was pushing herself too hard. Maybe she needed a break from all of this.

Chapter Sixteen

"**I** am telling you, Aunt Sharla. The girl, Dani said I look like her mom. At first, I was doubtful, but she showed me a picture, and it looked like one of those old pictures of Hannah with a hint of Monique and a dab of you."

They were sitting at the breakfast nook. Sharla had just come in from showing a house. She squinted at Giselle. "People look alike."

"I know but…" Giselle bit her lip. She didn't want to tell Sharla why she thought this was significant. She sighed. "I think God sent her."

"God?" Sharla raised an eyebrow, "as in creator of the universe?"

"Yes." Giselle nodded. "I was about to do something stupid in a weak moment. I thought I couldn't cope; I was telling God that he had to give me a definite miracle not to …" she cleared her throat.

"Oh Gis," Sharla reached across the table and squeezed

her hand.

"I am fine now." Giselle shook her head, "but I wasn't this morning. I am telling you, I felt rough. I was heading to my car when this girl bumped into me, stopped to talk, told me I looked like her mother, and then told me about some abortion debate she was going to participate in. I am a dead stranger, and that was the topic of conversation. Wasn't that a sign?"

Sharla nodded. "It certainly sounds like one."

"I have her number; she is expecting my call this evening. Her mom and dad own a business in Miami, but they are off on a cruise and won't be back until next month. They are a mixed-race couple like you and Tanner," Giselle said, "and her mother has Jamaican roots. Not Portland though—Trelawny."

"I see." Sharla seemed more interested now. "Trelawny?"

"You have any relatives in Trelawny?" Giselle asked.

"Not that I know of," Sharla said contemplatively. "But then again, I don't know my family history that well. We had some aunts and uncles on my father's side who lived in the hills of Portland. They didn't get on well with my father, so contact was limited. We had an aunt in Kingston named Maria, but she was even more of a black sheep than my dad. She was close to Hannah. She died before you were born."

"What about your mother?" Giselle asked. "I asked Jordan about her a couple years ago. He said that you were looking for her."

"Not really, I didn't pursue it." Sharla mused, "I had a conversation with one of my dad's sisters when I went to Maria's funeral. She was the only one who attended from that side of the family, and we got to talking. She told me a whole lot of stuff about their history. All ancient stuff about silly feuds that made no sense.

"Our family is fractionated. That is why I wanted something different for you and the boys. I wanted my sister's children to be close. So that we can be tighter knit unlike the frayed knots of the older generation."

Giselle nodded.

"Anyway, this aunt, I think her name was Mindy, mentioned that my dad would beat my mom within an inch of her life. She even speculated that he may have killed her and then said she ran away.

"I don't know if any of it is true. To my knowledge, my mother had no family except for us. I don't know what became of her after she left."

"Do you remember the beatings or abuse?" Giselle frowned.

"Faintly," Sharla sighed. "I remember that my mother was always crying. The sad part is I can't remember much else about her. I was five when she left."

"What was her name?" Giselle asked.

"Iris Kennedy. I think her maiden name was Baxter."

Giselle inhaled. "I used to think she was cruel for leaving her children behind when I heard her story."

"Maybe she didn't leave." Sharla had a pained expression on her face. "If my father got rid of her as my aunt said, the irony is he died a couple of months after she left. He ate green ackees and was poisoned."

Giselle drummed her fingers on the table. "Maybe I am treading the same path as Iris Kennedy. I am abandoning my baby."

"No, you are not." Sharla shook her head. "Yours is a totally different scenario. You are giving your baby to the father. And you will see him or her when you can. I don't think you should feel guilty about wanting to meet certain goals. Motherhood doesn't mean that your life has to end.

****

Dani became a fast friend to Giselle. She had a quirky sense of humor, and she loved babies. Her excitement when she found out that Giselle was having a baby was infectious.

She met Sharla and Tanner the day after their first encounter. Sharla liked her instantly.

"I hope she is a relative," Sharla said hopefully after they met. "I like her."

They sometimes met in the medical library. Dani was doing an undergrad degree in Human Biology. She was struggling with some of her courses, and Giselle was struggling in general.

Her first core class had her doing an absurdly hard research paper, and she just could not focus. All her powers of being in the zone and concentrating were shot.

By mid-February, she had concluded that pregnancy brain was a thing and she had it bad. She couldn't retain anything. She thought she had the brain of an elephant before, but she forgot everything now.

She was busy texting Pete instead of working. He insisted on day by day account of her pregnancy. There was nothing to report. She had it easy. She had even found out the sex of the baby after the scan.

She was having a boy.

A boy. One baby. She had been anxious about that. Her mother had multiples naturally.

"Is that your boyfriend?" Dani asked after she realized that Giselle was distracted.

"We broke up," Giselle said, looking up. "But he is very interested in the progress of the pregnancy."

"Ah," Dani raised an eyebrow. "You sure he is not

interested in you?"

Giselle looked down at her phone, at Pete's picture and inhaled roughly. He had not given her any indication for the past couple of weeks that he was interested in her personally. He kept his conversations strictly about the baby.

He was working on a major project at his new business and going to school too. He was just as busy as she was, if not more. He probably didn't miss her.

"You still love him," Dani broke into her thoughts. "I can see it stamped all over your face. Your eyes have that soft dreamy look. Why did you two break up?"

"Because of my plans for the future. This baby was not exactly planned." Giselle sighed. "I want to do tracks and have a career. I guess you can't have it all."

"I know some women who certainly try." Dani raised an eyebrow, "have you read about the virtuous woman in Proverbs 31. She sounds amazing. You can put your own personal spin on it. Don't worry, I will do it for you." Dani grinned. "I can't concentrate either. Your version goes like this:

"Who can find a woman like Giselle? For her price is far above rubies. The heart of her...what's your boyfriend's name again?" Dani asked.

"Peter, everybody calls him Pete, and he is not my..."

Dani held up her hand. "The heart of Pete doth safely trust in her so that he shall have no need of another. She will do him good and not evil all the days of her life. She winneth medals in the Olympics and finisheth her master's degree in Physiotherapy.

"She riseth also while it is yet night and studieth. She considereth a field, and beateth everyone in it: with the fruit of her hands she planteth a vineyard and starteth her own physio practice.

"She openeth her mouth with wisdom, and in her tongue is the law of kindness. She looketh well to the ways of her household, and eateth not the bread of idleness. Her children arise up, and call her blessed; Pete also, and he praiseth her."

Giselle chuckled. "I like you. You are just happy and motivating."

"It's the Christian meditation group I hang with in the mornings," Dani wriggled her brow, "I wasn't always this way, a friend of mine suggested it for my depression a year ago. That's when I joined them. I swear, when I stopped focusing on myself and the problems of this world and started focusing on God, I literally changed overnight. Maybe you should come."

"Sure," Giselle nodded. "I want that happy, positive attitude."

****

April rolled around with the swollen feet and the feelings of discomfort. She was definitely showing now. No doubt about it. She was heavily pregnant. She attended classes regularly, participated in group projects, did her light exercises, and went to Bible study.

It was a fifteen-minute program in the early morning on campus. At first, she had balked at the five-thirty morning meeting time, but she was used to training even earlier than that, and unlike training, it was quick and positive and left her feeling very upbeat for the day.

Miranda, the group leader, called it the secret weapon to survive the rat race. They usually sang uplifting songs and meditated on a scriptural passage. They had Giselle going home and reading the scriptures more closely.

It was becoming a habit, and she gradually realized that her tight-fisted approach to life was loosening up some. Maybe it was inevitable. Maybe it was the pregnancy. Maybe it was the fact that she was getting attached to her bump. She found herself reading to her belly.

Dani was the one who suggested it. She read textbooks and the Bible and rubbed her belly while she read, and she was becoming attached.

No doubt about it.

She wasn't so sure that she was going to just hand over her baby to Pete anymore. She had gone from not wanting to be a mother to become ridiculously sentimental. She didn't even know when the change happened.

Dani's mother Sara came over to meet them when she came back from her cruise and Giselle was a blubbering idiot by the end of the visit.

Sara had been adopted. She had no idea who her biological parents were. She was excited to meet them.

"I hope we are related." She kept repeating. "I've always felt like I am alone in this world. You know, biologically."

She and Sharla arranged to do a DNA test the next day.

When she left with Dani. Giselle was teary-eyed. She was not giving away her baby to anyone. Her baby was going to know her, and her baby was going to know Pete.

She called him to tell him of her change of heart.

He sounded groggy when he answered the phone.

"I changed my mind," She said it simply, no hellos, no fanfare.

"You changed your mind," Pete repeated.

"I am keeping the baby." Giselle sniffed, "I don't want to give away my baby. I love my baby. Did you know I almost did the abortion up here? I was so close, and God practically told me to stop. I am so glad he did because I do not want to part with my child. Nothing matters as much anymore.

Nothing at all, no training, no schoolwork."

She started crying. Pete heard her out.

When he finally spoke, his voice was husky, "Gis, I want to be a part of my baby's life too."

"I know." Giselle swiped her hand over her eyes. They felt gritty and swollen. "And that is why I am coming home. I can transfer my credits."

Pete was silent. "You are coming back home?"

"Yes." Giselle inhaled raggedly. "We'll have to work out something. We are going to be co-parents, after all.

Pete smiled. She could hear it in his voice. "I prayed this would happen. You are not as tough as you think you are, you know?

Giselle chuckled and then hiccupped. "No, I am not. I've been cut down to size. I am a mass of hormones right now. I cry over everything, even a bleach commercial. I can hardly see my toes, and I have heartburn."

"I wish I could see you. Touch your belly," Pete murmured and then cleared his throat. "Sorry."

It's okay," Giselle sniffed. "I'll send you a picture tomorrow. I met Sara today."

She talked with Pete way into the night without any significant pauses or uncomfortable silences, just like old times.

It felt good. She laid back in bed and looked up in the ceiling. Maybe the two of them had some kind of future. One could only hope.

Chapter Seventeen

"**W**hat are you going to name Baby Wiley?" Shawn asked Pete. He had been lost in coding, sitting in his new kitchen while his mom and Shawn, haggled over where they would put what. Both of them were hell-bent on decorating his new house.

"I, er, we were thinking Ethan Michael," Pete looked up from his screen. "Giselle thinks we should squeeze in Wilton from her father."

"Ethan Wilton Michael Wiley. I like it." Sheryl nodded. "My father's name was Michael."

"Yeah, I remember." Shawn started opening the kitchen cupboards one by one. "You are going to need kitchen utensils."

"I have him covered," Sheryl interjected looking around the all-white kitchen. "Giselle said her favorite color was grey and red. I know she won't live here, and they are so called on the outs, but I've been thinking about getting grey and red accessories."

"Oh yes," Shawn nodded. "That's a great idea I have the cutest red kettle and some red pots it doesn't fit in with my décor. I can bring them over. I like that you are just a five-minute walk from my place."

"I like this complex," Sheryl said. "It is really pretty. You are a talented architect, Shawn."

"Thank you." Shawn grinned. "Jordan gave me carte blanche on this one. I was going for environmentally friendly, green chic."

Pete listened to them as they rambled on, sometimes they asked him baby questions; sometimes they told him what they would be doing for him next. He was quite fine with both of them taking over his life. Shawn was on maternity leave, and his mother had stuck to him like glue these last couple of months.

She had even popped over to Florida last weekend to see Giselle.

"She is huge, and she is still studying and going to classes," Sheryl said as if reading his mind. "I booked Pete's ticket for the birth."

"Say what?" Pete blinked rapidly, "you didn't tell me any of this."

"I did." Sheryl frowned at him. "You said you wanted to go up for the birth and your father said we should go too, and we all agreed that we would go together. You need to hire a secretary at least for now, you are definitely going to need a nanny and a housekeeper if you are going to be a full-time father, businessman, and student."

Pete ran his hand over his face. "We do have a secretary for everyone at the office. Maybe I need a personal secretary. I'll ask Trish in HR to find me a nanny and housekeeper. She did a good job with the support staff we have now. We feel like a team now; we are getting stuff done."

"How are you handling all of that?" Shawn asked. "Whenever I see you, you are nose deep on that screen doing strangely magical things."

Pete chuckled. "I honestly can't keep up with the going to classes thing. I was talking to my faculty advisor the other day, and he recommended a good online degree. One that I can do at my own pace. I am going to do that because my Dad insists that I get myself a degree. Every Wiley male in this family is college educated, blah blah…"

Shawn grinned. "It's admirable that you still listen to your father even though you make your own money, have your own business and are about to be a dad yourself, bravo. How on earth did he become like this Sheryl? You do know he is exceptional."

"Yes, I do." Sheryl came over to him and kissed him soundly on the forehead. "If only he had listened when I said he should leave Giselle alone. At least until after he established his career had a couple of years when you two could get the breakup and makeup dance right and finally settle down into a mature, stable relationship. Why, oh why, don't children listen to their parents?"

"Not that again, Mom." Pete sighed. "You shouldn't tell people I told you so. Kick a broken man when he is down. I made my mistakes; I am living with them."

Sheryl squeezed his shoulders and stepped away. "I get spurts of disappointment I can't help it; I am a mother. I am the mother of an intelligent and handsome son; I was expecting you to get it right where your father and I failed."

Shawn cleared her throat. "Parents always expect the fairytale."

"You had the fairy tale." Sheryl reminded Shawn. "You were friends with Jordan, and then you married him, and now you have two lovely children."

"You have the fairytale too Sheryl. Besides, Pete still has time." Shawn looked across at him and smiled. "He and Giselle are just doing it in reverse."

"Don't have twenty children before you guys get married." Sheryl shook her head, "that would be veering far, far, away from the fairytale."

Pete chuckled. "Don't worry, I doubt that is going to happen. Giselle is not thinking about marriage. For right now we are talking. We are just friends who are going to have a baby together, and she is coming back here to live."

His phone rang just when he said that it was her. "I am going to have to take this."

"Tell her, hello," Shawn said. "and that I can't wait to meet Ethan Wiley."

Pete took the call on the patio. "Hey."

"Hey, you." Giselle said cheerfully. "Today, I learned that I have a new aunt. The results came back. Sharla and Sara are related."

"That means you and your new friend Dani are cousins."

"Yes!" Giselle squealed. "It is amazing! I don't think our meeting was a coincidence at all. God literally sent her in my life."

Pete smiled. He loved hearing Giselle sound optimistic and happy. It was as if she had taken a one hundred and eighty-degree turn since she told him she wasn't going to coldly hand over her baby. It felt like last summer after they had started to get close and then she went to Europe. He had missed her like an ache.

It had physically hurt him when she left. He was missing her like that now.

And she was coming back home.

A lot could happen when she came back home. They lived

in the same townhouse complex; they could see each other more often.

She would be in his house; he would be in hers.

But she was the same Giselle-ambitious and driven and self-focused. He wanted more from a relationship with her, he wanted to feel as if he came first. Anything else was a dud to him, he would never get in the way of Giselle's ambitions. He never wanted it to be said that he had held her back or impeded her dreams in any way.

When she came back, if she wanted them to get back together, she was the one who was going to initiate it. She was going to have to change, re-prioritize, because he was not going to be an afterthought with her.

He badly wanted them to work. He wanted them to be a family. A huge part of him wanted the fairy tale.

He listened to her talk, and he answered appropriately when he should.

"I miss you," He said it softly. He wasn't even sure that he had said it out loud until she stopped speaking, and then she finally said, "I miss you too."

****

Giselle had just finished her final exam when her water broke on her way to the car. She called her aunt to meet her at the hospital.

Sharla promptly called Pete, who was in the middle of a staff meeting.

"Giselle is having the baby right now!" Pete stood up a shell-shocked look on his face. "In less than a couple of hours, I am going to be a father!"

"Congratulations!" His team clapped. They seemed genuinely happy for him.

"I have to go." Pete picked up the phone. "Sorry about this guys. I need to make the next flight out of here. I want to be there when Ethan gets here."

"We'll just do what we discussed and pick this up when you get back," Rylee said.

She followed him out of the office. "I thought Queen Giselle wasn't going to give birth until later this month."

Pete glanced at her. "Well, our prince decided to come early."

"He'll probably look exactly like you. Preston Wiley clones." Rylee smirked. "The Wiley genes are strong."

"Maybe, maybe not." Pete hurried to his office. "I don't care how he looks; I just want him to be healthy."

"I saw Kurt last night," Rylee said, walking behind him. "You know his parents and mine are friends. They had a dinner, and we got to talking about you."

"Kurt, as in Kurt Yu?" Pete stopped.

"Yup. That's the one. What do you think of him?"

"Rylee, I am going to find a flight to Florida, I don't know what to tell you about Kurt right now. He is not exactly on my mind."

"He had a lot to say about you." Rylee patiently watched as he called his travel agent, jotted down the information for a flight leaving in two hours. He would have to rush to the airport.

When he looked up, Rylee was still there.

"Don't you want to know what Kurt Yu said about you?"

"I don't care," Pete said, grabbing his briefcase. "I don't give a flying hoot."

"He heard that Giselle is coming back to Jamaica."

"Uh…huh," Pete called his parents while Rylee watched him. He picked up his briefcase. "My dad is taking me to the airport."

"He wants to train Giselle again, and he doesn't know if you would be up for it. He thinks that you have the key to all that is Giselle and that you alone can determine what Giselle does when she gets here."

"I have the key to all that is Giselle?" Pete laughed. "If only that were true."

"He says she has always been in love with you, that for as long as he's known her it has always been you."

Pete narrowed his eyes at Rylee. "Why are you suddenly Kurt Yu's advocate? What does he want?"

"I like him." Rylee chuckled. "And he wants you to convince Giselle to train with him again when she gets back out here. She is no longer taking his calls."

"I have to go to my place and pack really quickly." Pete looked at Rylee. "Tell Kurt that Giselle will do what she wants to do. If I ever find this mythical key, I'll let him know."

Rylee nodded. "Okay, I'll tell him. Congrats again, Big Daddy. I am almost a teensy bit jealous of how happy you are right now."

****

Pete reached the hospital an hour before Ethan made his appearance in the world. He was the one who cut the umbilical cord. He was the first one to hold his son, a squalling bundle of preciousness, with all his fingers and toes, a healthy pair of lungs and a mass of curls.

"He is beautiful," Pete said. "Thank you."

Giselle nodded tiredly. His thank you was heartfelt, and they both understood why he said it.

"I am happy you are here for this."

Pete handed her the baby and Giselle stared down at his

precious, perfect face and realized that all the nonsense she had spouted about not wanting to be a mother and how she had other priorities was just that, nonsense.

Things had changed. Something had shifted in her. She was not the same girl who had entered the hospital. Things were different. Way different. She touched his soft miniature fingers and gazed at him for as long as she could. She was happy that he was here. She didn't have to learn to love him. She already did.

Chapter Eighteen

They settled in a routine quickly. Sharla spent one month with her and Giselle was grateful for that. She was inundated with new mom advice from the Wiley women and Georgia and even Elsa and Tiana who were reading one book after the other about newborns and what they should be doing and what she should be doing. She was definitely not alone in her motherhood journey, and it wasn't as hard as she thought it would be.

She and Pete had a schedule which Giselle was convinced kept them sane. She had so many volunteers to spend time with Ethan, she was beginning to believe she wasn't spending enough time with him on a one to one basis.

Shawn especially was a regular visitor; she had taken a year's maternity leave, and she had loads of free time on her hands. She came over regularly with her son, Cairo.

"He looks more like my husband than our own son," Shawn said, staring at the baby. "The resemblance is so uncanny. I could stare at this little guy all day. He is adorable. People are going to be confused when we take him out with us. They are going to think he is mine. You know what, let me have him."

Giselle laughed. "Shawn, you are so funny."

"You know what is funny," Shawn chuckled. "I never thought I would be the motherly type of person but here I am with two, and I was saying to Jordan the other day, we should just go for three or four, I am not getting any younger."

Giselle widened her eyes, "three or four?"

"Yes." Shawn grinned, "Ethan will need many playmates. Since you are going to have just one…"

"Just one? I don't know about that." Giselle frowned, now that she had Ethan, and she loved him so much, having more than one child was not a bad idea to her.

She told Tiana about the conversation when she came to visit in the evening.

So does this mean you are not going to do athletics again?" Tiana asked, sprawling out on her couch tiredly.

"I don't know." Giselle shrugged. "My priorities changed. Kurt calls me every other day, begging me to come back to the club. I told him I am just enjoying being a mother for now."

"So what about you and Pete?" Tiana asked. "You guys back together?"

"No." Giselle frowned. "It's all about Ethan for the two of us now. We haven't discussed our relationship or anything romantic. We are friendly, though. He is busy."

"So aren't you bored?" Tiana asked, "I never in a million years would expect that you would be the zen stay at home mom type."

"I am not." Giselle shrugged. "That's why I am going back to school in September. I already discussed it with Pete.

Sandrene and Aisha share a nanny, Shawn will be joining them soon when she goes back to work.

"The nanny lives at Guy's house, and she takes all the children when the Wiley women go off to work. It's convenient, she is right there in the Complex, and she is legit, Saint did his checks."

"But you are still nervous." Tiana grinned, "because you don't want to leave your son."

"That's true." Giselle nodded. "So true. She has a certificate in early childhood development, and she worked for some high-profile families in the UK and Sandrene loves her to bits but…"

"Really? So why is she out here?" Tiana asked skeptically.

"She is er white," Giselle said.

"So, what does that have to do with anything?" Tiana asked.

"She got pregnant for a black man while she was on vacation out here and when she went back home, her husband was not too pleased when the baby was born. It was obvious that he didn't belong to him.

"So she came back to Jamaica with her son and found out that her black lover was not exactly the most faithful or upstanding citizen. So she ventured out on her own." Giselle took up the baby monitor, "Is he sleeping too soundly. I don't hear sniffles or anything."

Tiana grinned. "You are obsessed, tell me more about the babysitter. Her story could be a novel."

"Nanny. She is a nanny."

"Okay, nanny, …whatever."

"That's all Shawn knows, but the most important thing is, she is legit, and she will be Ethan's nanny when I go back to school. He will be in a place with his family members and cousins."

"Yep, sounds like a good arrangement." Tiana nodded. "What's her name, the nanny?"

"Lizette Morgan." Giselle got up and stretched, "I am going to check on Ethan. I don't hear sniffles."

"Lizette Morgan! Tiana squealed. "That's James Dalton's mother!"

"James Dalton, high school teacher with the green eyes and killer bod, that you got fired?"

"That's the one." Tiana nodded.

"How would you know his mother's name?"

"Saw it on his next of kin when I er might have come across it in the admin office while I was er…"

"Stalking him?" Giselle chuckled. "It might be true; Liz has green eyes, and she does have a son. It may be her, as well as it might not be. Chill out Tiana. James Dalton is not around every corner waiting to exact revenge on the girl that got him fired, ended his engagement and got him thrown out of his home."

"It was school accommodation. He would have been thrown out anyway." Tiana growled. "Don't tell Liz Morgan my name just in case."

"I won't." Giselle grinned, "I don't want her to refuse to take Ethan. As of now, I am a twin. My twin's name is Elsa, you do not exist.

Tiana laughed. "I don't want you to lie, just don't mention my name, if you interact with her."

****

Pete was sitting in his office, staring at a string of code when his phone rang.

"Kurt is here to see you," Rylee said. "Please talk to him."

Pete sighed. "Okay, whatever."

He hung up the phone and stared at the code again.

"You know I never thought that I would be here, groveling at the feet of Peter Wiley, in his office."

Pete looked across at Kurt and grinned. "Have a seat, Kurt. I remember you being very snarky to me whenever I see you, so I know this must be important. What can I do for you?"

Kurt sat down and crossed his arms. "I need you to encourage Giselle to come back to training. She listens to you more than she listens to anyone."

"You overestimate my influence on Giselle," Pete said, "I am not that important to her."

"Not true." Kurt shook his head. "You were important enough for her to have your baby. If it were some other guy, me for instance, she wouldn't have had that baby. Don't get it twisted Pete, you are the reason that Giselle does anything.

"Giselle and I dated for close to a year, we kissed once. I don't know how long you two have been circling each other, it feels like forever, but all you had to do was crook your little finger, and she was sleeping with you.

"She wants the commitment and the children and the whole nine yards with you, and I get that, but she doesn't have to give up on athletics. She could have made it work. She was this close to being in the history books," he pinched his fingers together, "this close. Her times are phenomenal and have only gotten better since you two got together this year. I have always known that you are the secret weapon. I may not have liked it, but those are the facts."

Pete was skeptical about Kurt's speech.

He was Giselle's secret weapon? If only it were true. The past couple of months, he had to admit that he had caught himself on more than one occasion wishing that they were a couple.

It was easy enough to fantasize about it. They had a baby

together; they synchronized their schedules, they saw each other most mornings, they had dinner together most nights. They went in and out of each other's place with ease. It was near enough to domestic bliss, without the marriage and the sex and the intimacy.

"Listen," Kurt said to him urgently. "I saw the potential in Giselle, and yes, I wanted to coach a star athlete, but I also want to see her shine. She has worked for this for most of her young life. Being a mother is not the end of all her ambitions. I refuse to believe that."

Pete rested back in his chair. "I'll talk to her."

Kurt looked at him intently. "Next year is the Summer Olympics, she needs to be back in training ASAP."

Pete nodded. "Okay."

Kurt stood up. "Then I guess I'll see her at the club next Monday then. Thank you."

"I just said I'll talk to her," Pete said. "I can't guarantee anything."

"Oh, she'll be there," Kurt said. "You are the captain of team Giselle."

Pete stared into space bemusedly after he left.

****

Giselle was in the kitchen when Pete let himself into the apartment that night. It was unusual for her to be alone in the evenings. Usually, a family member or two would be there.

"Hey," he said, sitting at the island. "How is it going? How is Ethan?"

"Ethan is finally knocked out after a day of adventure; we went shopping, and he watched me trying to make pasta from scratch. I saw a pasta maker on sale, and I bought it."

Giselle said gleefully. "When I came home, I had to watch

a couple videos to perfect it, but here I am, a pasta chef. Now I am going to try to outdo myself on the sauce."

Pete smiled. "How much dough did it take to perfect it?"

"Quite a few batches but the end result is better than the stuff you get at the supermarket. It is off the charts good." Giselle looked up at him guiltily. "And here I was thinking that I was a reformed Type A personality."

"It takes time to reform a personality." Pete cleared his throat, "Gis, I saw Kurt today. He came to the office."

"Why?" Giselle asked.

"Because he thinks you have a shot at winning gold in the Olympics and he thinks you are throwing away all your years of training."

"Maybe I want to throw it all away. I almost killed my baby because of it. Whenever I look at Ethan, I think about how I was willing to delete him from existence all because of athletics and a stupid scholarship.

"Even you got the brunt of my ambition, I lied to you about the pregnancy, then I told you that he wasn't yours and I strung you out for weeks while I decided whether I would have him. I don't ever want anything to be more important to me than my child. I don't think I have the kind of drive in me anymore. Athletics and school had my entire energy."

"And now that you have your priorities in perspective," Pete said, "this should be easier, not harder. You can still achieve those goals, just not at the expense of your family. You'll just have to find the balance."

Giselle removed a tray of tomatoes from the fridge and stared at him. "Are you sure you are just nineteen years old?"

"Twenty in a couple of months." Pete grinned. "I am going to check on my son. Think about what I said."

"Thanks, Pete." Giselle leaned on the counter.

"And while I am feeling wise." Pete looked back at her,

"you need to forgive yourself for a couple months ago. Ethan is here now, and that is all that matters."

Giselle nodded. "Yes, that's true."

****

Giselle stretched and looked around. She had started classes in September. One of the hardest things was leaving her baby that first day back at school.

She had also started training in earnest.

But apparently not as earnestly as she used to. Kurt was frowning at her now.

"Earth to Giselle. I asked you a question."

Giselle blinked rapidly and focused on Kurt. "Sorry, what?"

"Are you doing Christmas camp this year? You need it."

"No," Giselle said quickly, "it's my baby's first Christmas. I have a million and one family events to attend. I even have new family. While I was in Florida, I discovered I had an aunt."

"Good for you." Kurt sighed. "Christmas camp would have given us a head start for next year."

"I know." Giselle shrugged, "but my priorities are different."

"I knew it would be." Kurt nodded. "Your times are actually not bad coming off your maternity leave. I didn't expect this; I am hopeful that you will get back to where you were sooner than I anticipated."

"Maybe." Giselle got up and stretched, "I don't focus on that anymore. It's not the absolute end of my world. I can quit this tomorrow and it wouldn't devastate me. I have my boys, Pete and Ethan."

She gasped when she said it and then looked at Kurt, her

eyes wide.

"I really did mean that."

"I know you did, and I am happy for you but don't talk about quitting. Next year is the Olympics and the year after that the World Championship. You will finally get your chance to shine."

"And yet that does not faze me one bit." Giselle grinned.

"Give me two years, Gis," Kurt said. "Just two, and then you can retire on a high."

"I don't know." Giselle shrugged, "we'll see."

She looked at her watch. "I have to go. I haven't seen the sweetest little boy in the world for too long."

"He is sweet, you and Pete made a very handsome baby together," Kurt said wistfully. "So how are you two working out?"

"We are good." Giselle tried to keep the optimism in her voice.

They shared a housekeeper and a nanny. It was less than a minute to walk from her place to Pete's. They were constantly at each other's house, but Pete had wrapped himself up in a bubble.

He wasn't the same with her. He talked with her, he laughed. He even stayed at her place until late, and they would watch a movie together, but he was keeping his distance, and it was obvious.

But she didn't want him to keep his distance. She wanted more.

Much more. She wanted them to be a family.

She wanted the commitment and togetherness. She wanted what she had always thought that she couldn't have—a family with Peter Wiley.

She headed to the shower. Her mind churning over. How was she going to win back Pete's affections?

Did he still find her attractive? The way he was acting, it was hard to tell. Was he seeing Rylee? He never discussed Rylee or his work life with her. Had she waited too long to tell Pete how she felt?

She shoved her bag into her locker more forcefully than needed.

"Somebody got on your bad side." Amara drawled.

Giselle spun around. "No, I was just thinking."

"I know the feeling." Amara nodded. "My locker door is damaged from my thinking too."

Giselle smiled.

"I was watching you out there." Amara said wistfully. "You came back with a vengeance, didn't you?"

"I did." Giselle nodded. "It seems as if a baby does change things."

Amara nodded. "Well, in your case, your changes are for the better. How is your baby?"

"He is the best baby in the world. Sometimes I can't believe that he is five months old already. I am still breastfeeding; I want to do that for as long as I can…"

Amara slumped on her locker and groaned.

"You okay?"

"I am good." Amara inhaled raggedly. "Envious. Wish I could time travel and do the right thing like you did."

Giselle nodded. "Thank you for encouraging me to keep him. He is the best gift I have ever gotten."

Amara nodded. "Yeah, I saw the picture on your Whatsapp. He is adorable. He looks like his dad."

"That he does." Giselle nodded. "But I see a hint of me in there somewhere."

Amara smiled. "Maybe the hair and the eyebrows."

"Yes. Giselle patted her on the back before she left. "You know what someone said to me the other day?"

"What?" Amara asked.

"You need to forgive yourself." Giselle patted her on the hand.

"I ah…," Amara blinked rapidly, "It's a work in progress."

****

Pete was at home when she got there. He was lying on the settee with Ethan on top of him fast asleep. He had his eyes closed and the radio was on, so low she couldn't hear what was playing.

She stooped down beside the two of them. They were her world, there was nothing more precious to her. They were her first priority. Tears sprang to her eyes.

Pete and Ethan. Ethan and Pete.

She sat on the floor and watched them.

Pete slowly opened his eyes and saw the tears on her cheeks. "What's wrong?"

"I just realized that I am stupid." Giselle sniffed. "I love you, and I want to be with you, and nothing else matters."

Pete sat up slowly. "I am dreaming, aren't I?"

"No. Giselle swiped her eyes.

"Let me put him down," Pete whispered. He headed up the stairs and then came back quickly.

"Gis…"

"Yes," Giselle looked at him. "I've been selfish, and one track minded, and it just hit me. I don't want to be like that anymore. I'll give it up, I'll give it all up if you want me to."

Pete crouched down beside her and smiled. "Gis, are you offering to give up on your dreams for me, for us?"

"Yes," she hiccupped.

"I'd never ask you to do that." Pete cupped her chin and looked at her intently. "Thank you for offering, but your dreams are part of who you are. All I want is for us to share your dreams together. Put each other first. I think if we do that, that's half the battle won, okay."

Giselle flung her arms around him.

"By the way, I love you too," Pete said in her ear. "I always have, and I always will."

He pulled away from her slightly. "I have a ring, I bought it almost a year ago. I want to do an official proposal."

Giselle wiped her eyes. "Okay. Yes. I'll marry you."

Pete laughed. "Shouldn't I propose first?"

"We are long past that." Giselle grinned. "I want a quick wedding. Suddenly I want to be Giselle Wiley so bad. I also want another baby, maybe after the Olympics."

She shook her head. "Sorry, here I am being selfish again. What do you want, Pete?"

Pete laughed. "I want exactly what you want."

Epilogue

One year later…

It was tense inside the Wiley Complex. Everybody gathered around Walter's large screen television for the watch party.

"I can't watch this." Sheryl got up and started pacing.

"Me, neither." Tiana got up with her.

"Will you two come and sit down. Preston asked, annoyed. "Giselle is in the finals of the Olympics. It is not brain surgery. Even if she doesn't win, we will be happy and celebrate. She is top eight in a hard field. It was a long hard fight to be where she is now."

"We are proud of our girl." Guy pumped his fist.

"There is Pete with the flag!" Jordan laughed. They panned into Pete again, and the Wiley clan started clapping.

"Ethan, there is your daddy." Sheryl went for Ethan in his playpen to distract herself.

"Sheryl, leave Ethan alone." Preston laughed, "you might drop him when you start to celebrate."

Sheryl grinned. "Maybe, you are right."

Ethan chortled. He looked around and clapped his hands. He was oblivious to the reason for the excitement around him.

When the start gun went off, everybody was silent. Giselle cleared her hurdles flawlessly and then came into the home stretch; she was clearly in front of the field.

Pandemonium broke out when she crossed the finish line first. There was not one dry eye in Walter's living room when she won.

After she won, they did the obligatory interview.

"Giselle Wiley, your story has been one of the inspirational ones this year. You came back from having a baby to dominating the world stage. Some people said it couldn't be done but you were the one to beat on the circuit this year, and you came here and proved that it was not a fluke. You are an inspiration to working mothers and female athletes who are looking to make a comeback. What do you have to say?"

"Trust God." Giselle panted in the mike. "I did, and he brought me through. I also would like to credit my husband Peter; he was and has always been my rock. My coach Kurt Yu, and my family for this win. It truly takes a village with me, and I am especially dedicating this win to my baby boy, Ethan. I love him with all my heart, and I am thankful that I had him. I would not exchange him for anything in this world."

"There you have it ladies and gentlemen, Olympic gold winner and proud new mom, Giselle Wiley."

Giselle blew a kiss in the stadium stands to Pete, who was cheering wildly. He had on a shirt with the slogan Team Giselle.

"Love you, babe." She mouthed to him.

"Love you too." He mouthed back. Somebody handed her

a flag, and she did her victory lap.

Kurt, who was standing beside Pete. Turned to him, happy tears streaming down his face.

"We did it!"

"Yes, we did." Pete chuckled.

"You and Ethan are the best thing that ever happened to Giselle."

And that was the unvarnished truth.

The End

Author's Note

Dear Reader,

Thank you for reading Baby For A Pryce. We got to spend time with the Wiley's again! Did you see how the family is growing? And can you imagine that Preston Wiley is a grandfather?

Anyway, I know it was not about the Wiley brothers, but it was nice getting into the Wiley world once more.

As for Giselle and Pete, I think they are perfect together and will remain happy together. After all, Giselle is working on her balance and she knows what is really important in her life. Tiana's story is next. An excerpt of Right Pryce, Wrong Time is on the next page.

As usual, thank you for reading my work.

All the best,

Brenda

Here is an excerpt from Right Pryce, Wrong Time
(Pryce Sisters Book 2)

"Tiana Pryce, you will not believe this!" Carla entered the office that they shared waving a piece of paper.

"What?" Tiana looked up from her laptop. She was editing the most boring law textbook ever written. She was convinced that the professor who wrote it seriously hated his students and wanted them to suffer.

"My cousin Minka who works at JD Productions in California just gave me the best news! The best!"

"She won the lottery, and she is giving you half?" Tiana grinned. "Congrats!"

"No." Carla chuckled. "That would be good news, but I don't like free money. I like to work for it, but this news is like winning the lottery."

"Okay, I'll bite." Tiana grinned. "What is it?"

"I am so happy I cannot speak! I need this to sink in." Carla plopped herself in her chair and pinched herself. "Tell me this is not a dream!"

"It's not a dream," Tiana said, leaning forward in her chair, "I can't wait to hear what has you so breathlessly excited."

Carla fanned herself dramatically. The air conditioner was high enough that fanning was unnecessary, but Carla seemed like she needed to do something with her hands. She was hyperventilating.

Carla took a deep breath and then another. "Okay, so, I didn't tell you this, but I've been sending Minka scripts to sneak into her boss. She's a production assistant on the show Secrets of Love."

"Which you are obsessed with." Tiana supplied.

"It finally worked; the writers are going to use one of my

scripts for season five!" Carla said in a rush. "They want to fly me over there to work on season five with them. Me, Carla Lindsay! I am gonna work on Secrets of Love. My words will be in the mouths of the actors. My thoughts will be brought to life. My name will be on the screen!"

"Are you serious?" Tiana squealed. "Seriously!"

"Yes," Carla gasped. "I absolutely can't believe it.

"You will have to pause the credits at the end to see your name," Tiana said enviously, "but still, that's great. A writer's dream. My dream."

"I know," Carla blinked her eyes rapidly, "I am… what's the word that Mr. Oliver likes to use?"

"Gobsmacked," Tiana said faintly. "Wow, I am jealous and happy for you at the same time."

"No need for jealousy, Missy." Carla smiled. "I have good news for you too."

"They want me to work on Secrets of Love?" Tiana widened her eyes. "I don't even watch the show anymore. I stopped when they killed off the hotel doctor. He was the one who was solving all the clues. He was the reason why I watched it in the first place."

"He was a villain." Carla grinned. "They have a new villain every season. Anyway, they brought him back as his twin brother, and it is even juicier than season two, the twin brother was seeing the hotel manager."

"Goodness." Tiana grinned. "Talk about a plot twist."

"Anyway," Carla said, "we were talking about your good news."

"Yes," Tiana nodded eagerly.

"They will be filming a soap opera here in Jamaica. Minka said it's a period piece. I don't know what it's about, and I don't know where the filming location will be, but the showrunner for Secrets of Love is in Jamaica to add to the writing team for that show."

"Get out of here!" Tiana gasped. "That's awesome."

"Yup." Carla nodded, "I am almost persuaded to give up my beloved Secrets of Love for this new project, but the thing is, I am not sure if I would get a shoo-in for this. Minka said more that forty writers have applied for it already, but they only need two from the pool. It will be a vigorous interview process and apparently you have to know 1800s Jamaican history."

Tiana made a face. "There goes my hopes, I am just an amateur I won't get a shoo-in."

"Don't say that yet." Carla handed her the paper. "They are still taking manuscripts, to assess who they should shortlist. Unfortunately, the deadline is today."

Tiana took the paper from her and scanned it. "You need to send a sample of your writing to Traci Pink at JD Productions."

"Yup, that's the showrunner's assistant." Carla nodded, "Minka says she is brutal."

Then you are required to spend three weeks somewhere in St. Ann where they put you through a series of pressure tests, writing obstacles where one person will be eliminated until they reach the final two." Tiana looked up, "what kind of a job interview is this?"

"Sounds good to me," Carla said. "They have to be thorough, make sure that you can work with the writing team or that you can actually write. It's a great opportunity. I'd do it for the competition alone."

"Yes, I know you love competition." Tiana frowned, "but I don't."

"You must absolutely enter," Carla insisted, "you complain every day about your job here. Neither of us like non-fiction, you should try to do something that you like. I know you are a great writer, that novella you wrote about the teacher was perfect. You should send that as your sample."

Tiana blushed. "I er think it needs work."

"It was good. I liked it. Once upon a time when Cannon Publishers took fiction manuscripts, I edited those." Carla grinned. "I think your story would sell. Take a chance, T. You shouldn't miss this opportunity. I know how miserable you have been lately."

"It's these law journals." Tiana rubbed the back of her neck. "I don't mind editing, I love it but this past year was one dry, thirsty, journal after the other with a thousand pages. Besides, there is no way Mr. Oliver will give me three weeks' vacation. I took a week to see my sister run in Europe. He grumbled the whole time he signed off on it."

"And though I am almost done with this boring monstrosity of a law book. I have the history tomes to get through. It's three volumes, and I have to double check dates and all of that…"

"So quit your job," Carla said flippantly, "chase that dream."

"Quit my job?" Tiana widened her eyes. "Quit my job! Are you crazy? I am saving up to buy a house."

"You can always come back with your tail between your legs if you fail." Carla rolled her eyes. "You know, Mr. Oliver has a soft spot for you. This place can always use one more editor. We have more manuscripts than editors for the next two years."

Tiana shook her head. "I don't know. I'll think about it."

"The deadline is today." Carla pointed at the paper. "You don't have a lot of time to think about it."

Tiana drummed her fingers on the desk. "Well…"

"It takes a lot of courage to release the familiar and seemingly secure, to embrace the new. But there is no real security in what is no longer meaningful. There is more security in the adventurous and exciting, for in movement, there is life, and in change, there is power." Carla read the quote she had posted above her desk.

"Andy Cohen knew what he was talking about," she flashed a grin at Tiana. "That's why I am quitting too, by the way. Already typed up the resignation letter."

Tiana grunted. "I am not you, Carla. I don't know, I don't know, I don't know…"

"You will get past round one," Carla said encouragingly, "enter the thing, send your Teacher Script. If they call you for the three-week interview you should go. Simple. You have to be in it to win it."

Tiana grabbed the paper again and typed off the email address. "I guess it won't hurt to send the sample. I can always beg for the three weeks from Mr. Oliver. That way if I am booted out in their elimination, I still have a job here."

"Yes, that's the spirit, send it, then forget about it," Carla said. "I will have to make plans to hand off my pile of manuscripts and alert HR to my imminent resignation."

"You know, I have been working with you for a year, and you never struck me as the type of person who would pull up stakes and leave it all behind."

Carla laughed. "People always read me wrong. I have a bookish air about me, but under this nerd exterior, there is a rabid adventuress. I am thirty-nine and single. Nothing is holding me back. I say seize the day."

"Seize the day." Tiana turned to her computer. "Okay, I am seizing the day. Carpe diem."

"I heard that the showrunner of Secrets of Love is scrumptious," Carla said after she sent the manuscript. "Minka says he is especially lovely to look at. How did she put it? He has the prettiest green eyes, the purest caramel complexion, and the pinkest most sensual lips. She thinks he should be in front of the camera, not behind it."

Tiana hit send and then jerked. That description could fit James Dalton down to the T.

"What's his name?" She asked her voice coming out in a croak.

"I don't remember," Carla said dreamily, "I was trying to envision what the combination of green eyes, dark skin, and pink lips would look like. Maybe Jesse Williams, that doctor from Grey's Anatomy? His eyes are green, right?"

"Don't remember," Tiana groaned. "Try to recall, Carla. What was the name of this showrunner?"

Carla closed her eyes dramatically.

"Was it, James?" Tiana looked at the monitor fearfully.

"Yes, that's right." Carla nodded. "James David, or was it, James Derrick. It was two first names."

"James Dalton." Tiana slumped in her chair, "JD Productions. Oh my word, I shouldn't have sent my manuscript then."

"Why not?" Carla asked. "Do you know James Dalton?"

"Oh, yes." Tiana nodded. "He was once my English teacher when I was in high school."

"That's great!" Carla grinned. "Were you a good student?"

"Well," Tiana bit her lips, "I would write the most elaborate essays."

"He'll shortlist you in a heartbeat then." Carla clapped, "you are his former student, how could he not?"

"Well," Tiana shook her head. "The essays I wrote were about him and me, some of them were pretty cheesy and outright erotic. I stalked him, got him fired from his job when I got one of my friends to take a picture of us kissing."

Carla widened her eyes. "What?"

"I had a gigantic crush on the man." Tiana sighed. "Let me

tell you, I had it bad. I had this idea to take a picture of us kissing, but then my phone got lost, and the principal of all people was the one who found it. She scrolled through my pictures hoping to identify whose phone it was, and what do you think she saw—one of her teachers in a compromising position with her student, he was fired the same day."

"Wow, that's tough." Carla shook her head. "Did he kiss you back?"

"No." Tiana groaned. "He was shocked at first, and then he was mad, especially when he saw Yara with my phone snapping away. I have never seen a person angrier than Mr. Dalton was that day. He thought I was out to ruin him.

"He hates me.

"Might as well get back to this law journal because there is no hope of me getting chosen for his writing team. Once he sees my name, my work is going to file thirteen without a doubt."

Fire and Walter (Book 3)- Walter's past came rushing to greet him shortly after his appointment as church elder. The new pastor was his childhood molestor, his wife was his ex from college and her cousin was the girl who got away. Walter had a lot of decisions to make.

The Perfect Guy (Book 4) - After a patient five years waiting for Lucia, Guy had his work cut out for him to prove himself worthy of her affections. He had played the part of poor farmer for too long and now he had competition in the form of the handsome doctor Ace Jackson.

The Patience of A Saint (Book 5)- Something was wrong with Saint's wife Sandrene. It didn't take a genius to see that she was changed beyond all recognition. Saint had to get to the bottom of it, before it was too late for them to salvage anything from the relationship.

A Case of Love (Book 6)- After a concert, Case is offered a girl to buy. Her fate was in his hands. He could keep her or leave her to the mercy of her evil family.

Resetter Series

Never Too Late (Book 1)- Addi finds out she is a resetter and goes back to the summer of 92 to change her family's lives.

Never Say Never (Book 2)- Skyler's handsome college lecturer, who happens to be her neighbor, has a 't' in his palms. Should she tell him the significance of it. If she does, would he believe her?

Now or Never (Book 3)- Ten years later Addi and Randy meet again at Randy's engagement party. Why is it that the chemistry between them was still so potent? Can they ever have a future together? Would Randy choose her this time around?

Almost Never (Book 4)- Tech genius Joshua Porter had all but given up on love. He then meets Portia, an inmate at the female penitentiary and his life takes a turn for the adventurous.

The Scarlett Family Series

Scarlett Baby (Book 1)- When the head of the Scarlett family died, Yuri had to return home to Treasure Beach for the funeral. What he didn't count on was seeing Marla, his childhood sweetheart and his best friend's wife. And when emotions overwhelm them and a few months later Marla is pregnant, Yuri wants the impossible: his best friend's wife and the baby they made together...

Scarlett Sinner (Book 2)- Pastor Troy Scarlett realizes the hard way that some sins are bound to be revealed, like the child that he had out of wedlock with his wife's mortal enemy from college. His wife Chelsea was not happy with the status quo. She was not taking care of the son of the woman she had so despised from college. And she could not get over the deep betrayal that she felt from her husband's indiscretion.

Scarlett Secret (Book 3)- Terri Scarlett had a soft spot for her friend, Lola. She was funny and sweet and they looked remarkably alike. But when Lola's Arab prince demands his bride, Terri foolishly exchange places with her friend and they meet up on a world of trouble.

Scarlett Love (Book 4)- Slater always looked forward to delivering packages to the law firm where he could get a glimpse of the stunning female lawyer, Amoy Gardener. Unfortunately, for Slater a woman like Amoy would not take him seriously, especially when she found out that he could not read!

Scarlett Promise (Book 5)- Driven by desperation Lisa Barclay decides to make some extra money by prostituting herself after being kicked out in the streets. Her first customer turns out to be a popular government senator and then to her horror he dies...

Scarlett Bride (Book 6)- When Oliver Scarlett's missionary work in the Congo region was coming to an end, he had a decision to make, marry Ashaki Azanga and save her from being the fourth wife to the chief of the village or leave her to her fate and get on with his life...

Scarlett Heart (Book 7)- After receiving a heart transplant shy librarian Noah Scarlett started to take on character traits that were unlike him and he kept dreaming of a girl named Cassandra Green...

Rebound Series

On The Rebound- For Better or Worse, Brandon vowed to stay with Ashley, but when worse got too much he moved out and met Nadine. For the first time in years he felt happy, but then Ashley remembered her wedding vows...

On The Rebound 2- Ashley reinvented herself and was now a first lady in a country church in Primrose Hill, but her obsessed ex friend Regina showed up and started digging into the lives of the saints at church. Somebody didn't like Regina's digging. Someone had secrets that were shocking enough to kill for...

Magnolia Sisters

Dear Mystery Guy (Book 1)- Della Gold details her life in a journal dedicated to a mystery guy. But when fascination turns into obsession she finds herself wanting to learn even more about him but in her pursuit of the mystery guy she begins to learn more about herself...

Bad Girl Blues (Book 2)- Brigid Manderson wanted to go to med school but for the time being she was an escort working for her mother, an ex-prostitute. When her latest customer offers her the opportunity of a lifetime would she take it? Or would she choose the harder path and uncertain love with a Christian guy?

Her Mistaken Dreams (Book 3)- Caitlin Denvers dream guy had serious issues. He has a dead wife in his past and he was the main suspect in her murder. Did he really do it? Or did Caitlin for the first time have a mistaken dream?

Just Like Yesterday (Book 4)- Hazel Brown lost six months of memory including the summer that she conceived her son, and had no idea who his father could be. Now that she had the means to fight to get him back from the Deckers, she finds out that the handsome Curtis Decker is willing to share her son with her after all.

New Song Series

Going Solo (Book 1)- Carson Bell, had a lovely voice, a heart of gold, and was no slouch in the looks department. So why did Alice abandon him and their daughter? What did she want after ten years of silence?

Duet on Fire (Book 2)- Ian and Ruby had problems trying to conceive a child. If that wasn't enough, her ex-lover the current pastor of their church wants her back...

Tangled Chords (Book 3)- Xavier Bell, the poor, ugly duckling has made it rich and his looks have been incredibly improved too. Farrah Knight, hotel heiress had cruelly rejected him in the past but now she needed help. Could Xavier forgive and forget?

Broken Harmony(Book 4)- Aaron Lee, wanted the top job in his family company but he had a moral clause to consider just when Alka, his married ex-girlfriend walks back into his life.

A Past Refrain (Book 5)- Jayce had issues with forgetting Haley Greenwald even though he had a new woman in his life. Will he ever be able to shake his love for Haley?

Perfect Melody (Book 6)- Logan Moore had the perfect wife, Melody but his secretary Sabrina was hell bent on breaking up the family. Sabrina wanted Logan whatever the cost and she had a secret about Melody, that could shatter Melody's image to everyone.

The Bancroft Family Series

Homely Girl (Book 0) - April and Taj were opposites in so many ways. He was the cute, athletic boy that everybody wanted to be friends with. She was the overweight, shy, and withdrawn girl. Do April and Taj have a love that can last a lifetime? Or will time and separate paths rip them apart?

Saving Face (Book 1) - Mount Faith University drama begins with a dead president and several suspects including the president in waiting Ryan Bancroft.

Tattered Tiara (Book 2) - Micah Bancroft is targeted by femme fatale Deidra Durkheim. There are also several rape cases to be solved.

Private Dancer (Book 3) Adrian Bancroft was gutted when he returned to Jamaica and found out that his first and only love Cathy Taylor was a stripper and was literally owned by the menacing drug lord, Nanjo Jones.

Goodbye Lonely (Book 4) - Kylie Bancroft was shy and had to resort to going to confidence classes. How could she win the love of Gareth Beecher, her faculty adviser, a man with a jealous ex-wife in his past and a current mystery surrounding a hand found in his garden?

Practice Run (Book 5) - Marcus Bancroft had many reasons to avoid Mount Faith but Deidra Durkheim was not one of them. Unfortunately, on one of his visits he was the victim of a deliberate hit and run.

Sense of Rumor (Book 6) - Arnella Bancroft was the wild, passionate Bancroft, the creative loner who didn't mind living dangerously; but when a terrible thing happened to her at her friend Tracy's party, it changed her. She found that courting rumors can be devastating and that only the truth could set her free.

A Younger Man (Book 7) - Pastor Vanley Bancroft loved Anita Parkinson despite their fifteen-year age gap, but Anita had a secret, one that she could not reveal to Vanley. To tell him would change his feelings toward her, or force him to give up the ministry that he loved so much.

Just To See Her (Book 8) - Jessica Bancroft had the opportunity to meet her fantasy guy Khaled, he was finally coming to Mount Faith but she had feelings for Clay Reid, a guy who had all the qualities she was looking for. Who would she choose and what about the weird fascination Khaled had for Clay?

The Three Rivers Series

Private Sins (Book 1) - Kelly, the first lady at Three Rivers Church was pregnant for the first elder of her church. Could she keep the secret from her husband and pretend that all was well?

Loving Mr. Wright (Book 2) - Erica saw one last opportunity to ditch her single life when Caleb Wright appeared in her town. He was perfect for her, but what was he hiding?

Unholy Matrimony (Book 3) - Phoebe had a problem, she was poor and unhappy. Her solution to marry a rich man was derailed along the way with her feelings for Charles Black, the poor guy next door.

If It Ain't Broke (Book 4)- Chris Donahue wanted a place in his child's life. Pinky Black just wanted his love. She also wanted him to forget his obsession with Kelly and love her. That shouldn't be so hard? Should it?

Contemporary Romance/Drama

After The End--Torn between two lovers. Colleen married her high school sweetheart, Isaiah, hoping that they would live happily ever after but life intruded and Isaiah disappeared at sea. She found work with the rich and handsome, Enrique Lopez, as a housekeeper and realized that she couldn't keep him at arms length...

Love Triangle: Three Sides To The Story- George, the husband, Marie, the wife and Karen-the mistress. They all get to tell their side of the story.

The Preacher And The Prostitute - Prostitution and the clergy don't mix. Tell that to ex-prostitute, Maribel, who finds herself in love with the Pastor at her church. Can an ex-prostitute and a pastor have a future together?

New Beginnings - Inner city girl Geneva was offered an opportunity of a lifetime when she found out that her 'real' father was a very wealthy man. Her decision to live up-town meant that she had to leave Froggie, her 'ghetto don,' behind. She also found herself battling with her stepmother and battling her emotions for Justin, a suave up-towner.

Full Circle- After graduating from university, Diana wanted to return to Jamaica to find her siblings. What she didn't foresee was that she would meet Robert Cassidy and that both their pasts would be intertwined, and that disturbing questions would pop up about their parentage, just when they were getting close.

Historical Fiction/Romance

The Empty Hammock- Workaholic, Ana Mendez, fell asleep in a hammock and woke up in the year 1494. It was the time of the Tainos, a time when life seemed simpler, but Ana knew that all of that was about to change.

The Pull Of Freedom- Even in bondage the people, freshly arrived from Africa, considered themselves free. Led by Nanny and Cudjoe the slaves escaped the Simmonds' plantation and went in different directions to forge their destiny in the new country called Jamaica.

Jamaican Comedy (Material contains Jamaican dialect)

Di Taxi Ride And Other Stories- Di Taxi Ride and Other Stories is a collection of twelve witty and fast paced short stories. Each story tells of a unique slice of Jamaican life.